"Sara," Mike whispered, "don't you think it's time you stopped hiding behind your kids?"

"I'm not," she protested.

He put his finger over her lips to silence her. "Do you realize this is the first time we've been alone? Really alone? Not just sneaking around while they're asleep or sitting outside the camper while you listen for the slightest sound."

His hand brushed aside some damp curls from her forehead. His touch was enough to shatter all her objections, but she had no voice to tell him so.

"You're a terrific mother, Sara, but you're also a woman. Let me get to know the woman, just like I've gotten to know the mother."

This time he did not give her a chance to speak, but brought his lips down gently on hers. His touch was magic, making her blood soar and her body turn to fire. It had been so long since a man had tried to please her. She wanted the pleasure to go on and on . . .

WHAT ARE *LOVESWEPT* ROMANCES?

They are stories of true romance and touching emotion. We believe those two very important ingredients are constants in our highly sensual and very believable stories in the *LOVESWEPT* line. Our goal is to give you, the reader, stories of consistently high quality that may sometimes make you laugh, sometimes make you cry, but are always fresh and creative and contain many delightful surprises within their pages.

Most romance fans read an enormous number of books. Those they truly love, they keep. Others may be traded with friends and soon forgotten. We hope that each *LOVESWEPT* romance will be a treasure—a "keeper." We will always try to publish

LOVE STORIES YOU'LL NEVER FORGET
BY AUTHORS YOU'LL ALWAYS REMEMBER

The Editors

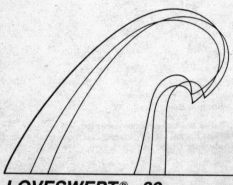

LOVESWEPT® • *89*

Anne and Ed Kolaczyk
Captain Wonder

 BANTAM BOOKS
TORONTO • NEW YORK • LONDON • SYDNEY • AUCKLAND

CAPTAIN WONDER
A Bantam Book / April 1985

LOVESWEPT® and the wave device are registered
trademarks of Bantam Books, Inc. Registered in U.S. Patent
and Trademark Office and elsewhere.

ISBN 0-553-21694-5

Published simultaneously in the United States and Canada

Bantam Books are published by Bantam Books, Inc. Its
trademark, consisting of the words "Bantam Books" and
the portrayal of a rooster, is Registered in U.S. Patent and
Trademark Office and in other countries. Marca Registrada.
Bantam Books, Inc., 666 Fifth Avenue, New York, New
York 10103.

PRINTED IN THE UNITED STATES OF AMERICA

O   0 9 8 7 6 5 4 3 2 1

To our own Kari and Megan
for all the wonder they've
brought into our lives

One

Sara Delaney held up two pairs of beaded mocca-sins. "How about these, girls?"

Her two eight-year-old twin daughters exchanged glances, then shook their heads in unison.

"Come on, Mom," Kari said. "You told us it was our money. Why can't we buy what we want?"

"And what's that?" Sara was almost afraid to ask.

Kari and Megan both reached for the T-shirt at the same time, but Kari got it first and held it up. Sara groaned when she saw the stern black and red clad figure staring back at her, his muscular arms akimbo, his eyes flashing with the help of some glitter, and that distinctive single blond curl dipping down over his forehead.

"Not Captain Wonder!" she cried. "I've finally saved enough money to bring us to the Grand Can-yon and you girls manage to find something with his picture on it. What's wrong with Indian moccasins?"

"They're just not awesome, Mom," Megan tried to explain.

"And Captain Wonder is?" She did not wait for an answer because she knew it all too well. Didn't Captain Wonder's heroic form protect Megan's lunchbox and adorn Kari's knitted ski cap and gloves? Wasn't it even on the nightshirt the girls had given her for her birthday last month? "I just wish you'd choose a souvenir that would remind you of our vacation, not something you could buy at home."

"But this will remind us of our vacation," Kari pointed out, "because he's here."

Sara stared in frustration at her daughters, tiny replicas of herself. The same dark hair, the same green eyes, and the same stubborn nature. Why in the world were they enamored of that muscle-bound creep? Why hadn't they inherited any of her good sense?

But the crowded gift shop was no place for a long discussion and the girls were right. It was their money. They had earned it weeding the garden and feeding the cats. They had the right to waste it on a dumb T-shirt if they wanted.

She picked out two medium-sized Captain Wonder shirts from the rack and carried them to the counter along with a pair of Indian moccasins for herself. The girls trailed behind, pointing wistfully to the Captain Wonder posters on the wall. Sara decided it would be wisest to pay quickly and leave, before they realized there were two posters they didn't have yet.

"Ooh, Captain Wonder. Isn't he the greatest?" The gum-chewing salesgirl sighed. "I mean, totally awesome."

Sara just smiled as the girls carefully counted out their money.

"Have you seen him?" the salesgirl went on, but this time recognizing the girls as her audience, not Sara. "I just missed him yesterday. He left the cafeteria about an hour before I got there, but I did get to sit at the same table he sat at. Maybe even in the same chair."

Kari and Megan sighed respectfully while Sara tried hard not to gag. Captain Wonder might be the hottest thing to have hit the television screen in the last ten years. He might have the power in his intense blue eyes to make women faint and evil-doers tremble, but she was fed up with him.

It wasn't enough that the girls had to watch his show every Sunday night. Now their first vacation ever had to be spoiled by him. This would have to be the week he chose to save the Grand Canyon from destruction. The whole place was swarming with his crew, his fans, and rumors of him. Just for once, she wished the bad guys would win. The world would be a more peaceful place without Captain Wonder, she thought. She took their packages and herded the girls out of the gift shop.

"I'm thirsty," Kari said as they passed the entrance to the cafeteria.

"There's a water fountain," Sara pointed out.

Megan frowned. "Mom."

Sara stopped walking and looked at her twin daughters. "I don't care if Captain Wonder did eat in the cafeteria yesterday. We do not have to hang around until he makes an appearance today. We must have hiked ten miles and I'm tired. I want to go back to the camper and rest." She saw the girls exchange glances. "And, no, you may not stay here by yourselves."

The girls sighed in disappointment, but followed their mother back out into the hot August after-noon. It was about a half mile from the lodge to the parking lot where their rented camper was wait-ing, and no one said a word the whole way. The longer the silence continued, the guiltier Sara felt. She couldn't have allowed the girls to stay there alone, but maybe she was forgetting that this was their vacation just as much as hers. It ought to be fun for all of them, no matter how she felt.

She unlocked the side door of the camper and pulled it open. "Instead of driving back to the campground now, why don't we stay here and eat at the lodge tonight? We can drive back after dinner," she suggested.

"Could we?" the girls asked together.

They immediately began planning what they would say to Captain Wonder when they saw him, for they were certain he would be sitting at the table next to theirs. Sara decided not to burst their bubble with reality, and went into the bathroom.

Had she ever been that young and romantic? It seemed impossible, but she supposed she had. Most girls went through a stage like that, dreaming constantly of their heroes. She couldn't remember mooning over some television hero when she was eight, but she suspected she had done a lot of dreaming about Tom. At least the girls could claim youth as their excuse; she'd had none. She'd been twenty when she married Tom, old enough to have known better, but she hadn't. She'd been forced to gain her wisdom the hard way. When she had divorced him a year and a half later, she'd felt like an old lady—worn-out and tired and highly suspicious of heroes.

Sara washed her face and hands and went out into the camper. In the little galley she found a bag of Snickers bars and offered them around. As she munched, she took her new moccasins out of the bag. They were soft buckskin with tiny beadwork nestled among the long fringes that ran around the top. She slipped one on and wiggled her toes comfortably. Then she slipped her foot into the other one. Or tried to, for it wouldn't go on. She peered inside and groaned when she read the tiny print. How had she done that? The left shoe was too full sizes smaller than the right. She'd have to go back and exchange it.

She looked over at the girls, but Megan seemed ready to fall asleep and Kari was trying to braid her hair. Neither showed any interest in walking back to the lodge, and Sara was relieved. She could go and come back a lot quicker on her own. So, after issuing strict instructions to the girls that they were not to leave the camper, she took off toward the lodge.

Michael Nathaniel Taylor tossed the black tights onto the pile of clothes with a sigh of relief. "My grandfather must be turning over in his grave every time I put those things on," he said wryly.

Norm, his manager, looked up from the pile of papers he was studying. "Why? He have something against being a millionaire?"

"No, he had a thing against men wearing tights." Mike pulled a robe around his body. "Besides, I always pictured myself as the rugged type."

"Millions of screaming teenage darlings all can't be wrong."

Mike grimaced. "I'm taking a shower. Captain Wonder is through for the day."

"Actually, he's through for the rest of the week," a voice called from the doorway.

Mike looked over at the woman who had just come into the room.

"We won't need to reshoot that fight scene after all. Everyone was satisfied with it, so you're through with all your scenes. You can spend the next few days signing autographs for all those teenyboppers."

"Just what I've always wanted to do," Mike said, then went down the hall toward the shower.

"Hey, don't knock it," Norm called after him. "You're thirty-four, remember? Pretty soon those sweet young things are going to notice your gray hairs and wrinkles. Then, when you're sitting alone in your rocking chair and gumming your oatmeal, you'll wish a few of those lovelies were still around."

Mike chose not to answer and closed the bathroom door. The role was easy and fun, and the money was certainly good, but he still felt stupid wearing those tights. Why couldn't he be a cowboy hero and wear blue jeans and boots? His father had done very well in westerns.

After his shower, Mike put on a pair of cutoffs and a plain T-shirt. Then he combed his blond hair in front of the mirror, trying to mash down that telltale Captain Wonder front curl so that it stayed with the rest of his hair. He frowned slightly at the less than hoped-for results, but gave up and jammed the comb into his pocket. It was the best he could do since his hair was deliberately cut to produce the effect.

He'd like to take a walk and see a little of the place, he thought. It was only Thursday and they weren't going back to Los Angeles until Saturday, but he wasn't eager to share the time with the hordes of adolescent girls swarming all over the place. Could he pass as an ordinary tourist without his tights and cape?

Mike stared thoughtfully at his image. His clothes were unexceptional and so was he. Out of his tights and with his curl disguised, he looked just like everybody else. He turned away, satisfied that he could blend into the crowds.

After putting on a pair of tennis shoes, he let himself out the back door of the trailer and hurried along the path behind the lodge. Two kitchen boys were tying up plastic garbage bags and looked up as he passed, but paid no attention to him. He put on his sunglasses, growing more confident with each step.

The area around the canyon itself was too crowded, so he chose a path that led away from it. A walk in the woods, away from the damsels in distress and threatening villains, would be relaxing.

He passed some people heading toward the lodge, but no one gave him a second glance. He straightened up from his unconscious slouch and walked more briskly.

Since he'd grown up and lived most of his life in Los Angeles, long walks in the woods were a rarity for him. Actually, any kind of long walk was a rarity for him these days. Since Captain Wonder's origin two years ago, he had become an instantly recognized figure and found his freedom restricted. Maybe that was why he had been so restless lately. Maybe Sylvia was wrong when she said he subconsciously wanted to marry her.

He shook her from his mind. It was good to be out on his own for a change. A late afternoon breeze ruffled his damp hair and he felt like running.

"That's him!" a young female voice shrieked.

Irritated that his peace and solitude had been suddenly shattered, Mike began to run. He had had enough of the fawning and pandering and just wanted to be left alone for a few hours. Damn. Was that asking for so much?

The path wove in among the trees, but the forest was not thick enough to hide him. Across the parking lot ahead, the woods seemed denser. If he could reach them before his fans reached him, he might have a chance to hide. He left the path and darted in among the bushes and trees. A branch scratched his cheek as he came out into the parking lot.

The squeals and shrieks were growing louder and closer. He felt as if the girls were hunters and he their prey. It was stupid of him to have run, it only made them more determined. He darted around a camper, hoping to find a path into the woods, then stopped abruptly. The camper door was open and two little dark-haired girls were beckoning him inside.

Mike didn't stop to think. He darted in and one

of the girls slammed the door shut. Then the three of them sat on the floor, their backs against the door. They held their breath as they listened to the conversation of his pursuers.

"Where'd he go?"

"He's got to be here somewhere. He couldn't have disappeared."

"Maybe he flew away."

The little girl with short hair giggled, but the one with long hair gave her a stern glance. Miss Short Hair became very quiet.

"Maybe he went into the camper."

Miss Long Hair leaned close to him. "You'd better hide in the bathroom." She pointed to a narrow door in a back corner of the camper.

It seemed like a good idea since he was in plain sight of the camper's numerous windows. He hurried into the tiny room and closed the door. A Captain Wonder nightshirt hung from the hook on the back and he frowned at it. Hiding in the bathroom suddenly seemed cowardly. What if the door wasn't locked and those kids got in? He had left those two little girls without much protection.

Before he had a chance to act, though, there was a timid knock on the door, and he opened it. The two little girls peered in. Their green eyes were wide and curious.

"They're gone," Miss Long Hair said. Miss Short Hair nodded.

"I certainly appreciate your help." He held out his hand. "My name's Mike."

The two faces fell as if they were one. "You're not Captain Wonder?"

He smiled. "Only when I wear my tights."

They looked relieved. "I'm Kari," Miss Long Hair said. "And that's Megan."

"You're twins."

"We know."

They looked so solemn, and he tried not to laugh.

"You hurt yourself," Megan told him.

He looked in the mirror and saw the scratch across his cheek. There was dried blood on it, but he barely felt it.

"Do you want a Band-Aid?"

He was about to refuse, but noticed their concerned faces. "If you have one," he said.

"I'll get it," Megan cried as she ran off.

Kari handed him a clean washcloth. "Mommy says you have to wash off your cuts."

"Good idea." He was carefully washing the dried blood off when Megan appeared with one Band-Aid. He smiled when he saw Snoopy on it. "What? No Captain Wonder Band-Aids?"

"Mommy said 'Absolutely not,' " Megan mimicked in a "grown-up" voice. " 'I will not have that man on everything in our house.' "

Kari looked worried that her sister might have offended him. "But she did let us buy Captain Wonder T-shirts instead of moccasins today."

"That was nice of her." Mike stared at his reflection in the mirror. With the orange slash bearing Snoopy across his cheek, he looked definitely unlike Captain Wonder.

"And she has a Captain Wonder nightshirt," Kari went on. "We gave it to her for her birthday last month. She was thirty."

"Auntie Jane says she should wear it inside out so that Captain Wonder will be closer to her heart," Megan confided. "But Mommy said—"

" 'Absolutely not,' " he finished for her with a laugh. "I can see why your mother didn't buy Captain Wonder Band-Aids. She has enough of him in her life already. Your father might think she likes Captain Wonder better than him."

"Oh, she does," Megan assured him.

Mike was not sure from the way she said it that it was a compliment.

"Yeah, she hates Daddy," Kari agreed. "She just doesn't like you."

"Oh." A small distinction, to be sure. "Well, I certainly do appreciate all your help, but I'd better be on my way." The sound of knocking on the door stopped them all.

"Kari! Megan! Open up, it's Mom!"

The girls exchanged worried glances. Then, without a word, Kari pulled the bathroom door shut in Mike's face, leaving him to stare at the Captain Wonder nightshirt. It was, he noted with growing curiosity, stretched out in all the right places.

Sara was in no mood to be friendly or even polite when she got back to the camper. She had not been able to get the moccasins she had wanted and had had to settle for her second choice. And because they were not the same price, she'd had to wait forever in line behind a herd of Captain Wonder fans. She'd had enough of teenage girls for one day and was not thrilled to see them hanging around the camper.

"Are you going in there?" one asked her as Sara knocked on the door.

Before Sara could ask her what business it was of hers, another sighed. "He's in there."

"He? He who?"

Their collective sigh was answer enough. "*He* certainly is not in there," Sara announced. "This is my camper and there are no *He*s here at all."

She turned to frown at the closed door. Where were the girls? "Kari! Megan! Open up, it's Mom." She knocked again, and suddenly Kari opened the door.

"Oh, hi, Mom."

She sounded strange, but Sara was more interested in shutting out the curious faces of the girls outside. "Lord, I can't believe this place," she said, putting her packages on the table and closing the drapes across the window above it. "Can you believe it? They actually think Captain Wonder's in here."

The girls exchanged worried glances and Megan suddenly became interested in her mother's shoes. "Did you get the ones that fit this time?"

"Yes, I did."

"Can we see them?" Kari asked, and looked into the bag. "Boy, they're really pretty. How do they look on you?"

"Like moccasins," Sara said dryly, looking from one girl to the other. Something was going on. What kind of plot had they hatched for dinner? "I made six-thirty reservations at the dining room. That sound okay?"

"Oh, sure. It sounds fine. Do you think those girls will still be outside then?" Kari asked.

"Does it matter?"

"No, I guess not."

Sara picked up her moccasins and her purse. "I think I'll wash up and then read a little before we go to dinner."

"Wash up?" Megan gulped. "Now?"

"Why not?"

"Well, *we* were just going to wash up, weren't we, Meg?" Kari nudged her sister.

"Yeah, we were."

Sara's eyes narrowed as she stared at her daughters. "You two, the grimy twins, were going to wash up without being told? Just what is going on? Have you girls been into my makeup again?"

They shook their heads silently, but Sara did not miss the glance they exchanged. If it wasn't her makeup, then what? She looked around the eating area of the camper. Nothing seemed out of place.

"You girls want to tell me what's going on? Did you leave the camper while I was gone?"

"Oh, no, Mom."

Sara pulled open the cabinets, but everything was fine. The closet seemed undisturbed, so that left only the bathroom. She pulled open the door and found a man sitting on the edge of the sink. There was something terribly familiar about that curl dipping down over his forehead.

"Hi."

It was him. She had spent enough Sunday nights listening to that voice to be certain. Now she'd found Captain Wonder in her sink. He straightened up with a smile, as if lurking in people's bathrooms was his usual occupation.

She turned around. The girls were watching her with worried looks on their faces. "Might I have an explanation?" she asked.

"It was all my fault," he hurried to tell her.

Sara barely spared him a glance. "Always to the rescue, aren't you?" Her gaze went back to her daughters. "Well?"

"We had to, Mommy," Megan said. Kari nodded. "It was just like when we found Toby. You said it was our duty to save him."

"He"—she nodded toward the muscular blond who now stood in the doorway—"was in a garbage can and some boys were throwing rocks at him?"

"Well, sort of," Kari said.

"Teenage girls can be just as vicious," Captain Wonder pointed out. "They truly did save my life."

His voice had a richer quality than it seemed to have on television, and was much more disturbing. She moved a few feet away from him for her own sanity, and caught sight of his fans outside straining to see through the windows. If they saw him, they'd never leave, she decided.

"You'd better get back in the bathroom," she snapped, and went back to the door. "Girls, close all the drapes, will you?"

They raced to do her bidding as she let herself out. At the sound of the door opening, the teenagers rushed around to that side of the camper.

"When is he coming out?" one cried.

"He is not coming out because he is not in there," Sara lied. "Now, will you please leave? My husband and I find it very disturbing to have you peering in the windows."

"Your husband?" They looked at each other, clearly confused. "I was so sure it was him."

"Well, it wasn't," Sara said. "Now will you leave?"

She waited to see that they were starting back across the parking lot before she went back in. Captain Wonder was out of the bathroom, and the twinkle in his eyes told her he had heard her words.

"Thanks, dear," he said.

"Don't press your luck." He was larger than he ought to be and his presence seemed to fill the camper, making her feel smaller than her five-foot-two. All too conscious of his presence, she turned back to the girls. "I've had it for today. We are going back to the campground. We'll pick up something simple for dinner and cook it in the camper."

The girls watched Captain Wonder with questions in their eyes.

"We'll drop him off at the lodge as we leave," she said, trying to avoid looking at him. Her attempt failed miserably; there didn't seem to be anywhere else to look.

"I have a better idea," Captain Wonder said. "Why don't I take you all out to dinner? Not here because I'd get recognized, but someplace quiet, away from the park."

His smile reminded Sara of the girls when they were up to mischief, and her first instinct was not to trust him. But the girls looked so hopeful, the refusal died on her lips. Wasn't she letting her dislike of him cloud her mind? After all, their budget didn't run to steaks and a wine list. A change from hamburgers would be nice. And if she gave the girls an evening with Captain Wonder, they'd probably be in seventh heaven for the next few days and never think to complain about the old Indian sites she wanted to visit.

"Thank you," she said politely, squelching the sudden misgivings that filled her when she looked into his eyes. "We would be pleased to have dinner with you."

Two

"I'm sure 'Ted's' can't be much further."

Sara glared briefly at the blond man sitting next to her, then turned back to her driving. He had been assuring her for the last half hour that the restaurant was "just down the road," but it had yet to appear.

Actually, very little had appeared: two souvenir stands and the campground at which they had a site reserved. She was beginning to think that they should have braved the crowds at the lodge. If his adoring fans had gotten too pesky, she and the girls could have moved to another table.

She paused for a moment. Well, *she* could have moved. She was not at all certain that the girls were concerned with anything as mundane as dinner. It was more than an hour past their normal mealtime, and she hadn't heard the slightest complaint. They must be in love, she thought.

"That must be it."

For a split second Sara feared he really could

read minds, but then she realized that he was referring to the huge neon GAS sign up ahead.

"I thought we were filling our stomachs, not the camper."

He grinned at her. It was a heart-stopping sight, she admitted, but it had little effect on her. Hunger was a more primitive force.

"It's right next to the gas station. See, there's the sign."

Sure enough, there was a tiny sign that said "Ted's" over the gas sign. She hoped there was no special meaning in the respective sizes of the signs, and pulled into the parking lot. The juicy steak she had been dreaming of faded away when she saw the run-down building with its promises of "Fast Food" and "Cold Beer." She just hoped that there was still enough peanut butter left in the cabinet to make three sandwiches. Captain Wonder could fend for himself.

"Is this it?" Kari asked, peering over her mother's shoulder. Her voice was polite, but disapproving.

"Hey, it'll be great," Captain Wonder assured her. "No one will recognize me and we'll have fun."

It was obvious that his smile wiped away all of Kari's doubts, but it worked no such magic on Sara. She took Megan's hand and followed them into the restaurant. The place was just as she expected: a luncheon counter down one side of the room and a few Formica-topped tables in neat rows. A blaring jukebox serenaded the handful of customers.

Captain Wonder led them to a table in one corner and passed out the plastic-covered menus. Sara's was sticky.

"This is wonderful," she said.

This time just his eyes smiled at her, enfolding her in a gaze of astonishing intimacy. Her racing heartbeat took her by surprise, and she quickly returned her gaze to the menu. She was not an eight-year-old to be swept away by a guy who wore tights and flew.

"What do they have?" Megan asked.

"Hot dogs," Sara suggested.

"How about chili?" Captain Wonder offered.

"Is that what you're having, Mike?" Kari asked.

"Yep." He pointed to a spot on her menu. "See, right here. 'He-man special.' "

"It doesn't say that," she argued.

"Close enough."

Megan closed her menu. "I'm going to have what Mike is having."

"You hate chili," Sara reminded her.

"I'll have it too," Kari decided.

Sara's frown took them all in. "Look, just because Cap—" She stopped. Why did she keep thinking of him as Captain Wonder? She knew his name was Mike. The girls could say it. Why couldn't she?

Maybe it was because Mike was a sane name. A normal name. But this was a guy who stopped bullets with his bare hands. Who had a body no mortal man ought to be allowed to possess. This was not a Mike.

She cleared her throat and began again. "If you order it, you have to eat it," she said briskly.

"Do you promise to eat all the chili?" Mike asked the girls. They nodded. "No matter how ghastly it is?"

Megan hesitated. "What if some bad guys put poison in it?"

"I'll test it first. If I say it's safe, you have to eat it." He leaned closer to them conspiratorially. "Besides, we all know that chili is the food of superheroes. If you eat enough of it, you get as strong as I am."

They giggled as the waitress came over to take their orders. Sara asked for a hot dog, then paused for the girls to give their own orders. They had been ordering for themselves for the past year and did a nice job. The elderly waitress thought so too.

"Such well-behaved little ladies," she said with a sigh after she wrote down their orders. Sara smiled up at her and noticed she was staring at Mike. "You must be real proud of them."

"They're mine," Sara said quickly, then instantly wished she'd kept silent.

The waitress looked from one to the other, obviously confused. Mike jumped into the awkward silence with an easy smile and ordered his chili. His poise made Sara feel even more of a fool. Why had she done that? What difference did it make if some woman they would never see again thought they were a family?

It was just that the girls were hers. Hers and hers alone. Tom had left when they were four months old and she had raised them by herself. She was the one who'd sat up at night with them when they were sick, and then gone to work the next morning. She was the one who'd kept them fed and clothed and happy and who had finally managed to make a down payment on that two-bedroom town house. Her first, instinctive reaction had been plain old jealousy. Unfortunately, her second reaction, a more reasonable one, had arrived a bit too late to stop her from acting on the first.

She bit her lip and looked around the table, aware that she had dampened everyone's spirits. After taking a drink of water for courage, she forced a smile onto her face. "Weren't your parents in show business, Mike?"

He nodded. "My dad starred in over forty westerns. I had bit parts in a few of them."

"What's a bit part?" Kari asked.

"Just a small role. I usually led the horse off to the stables or something like that. They never gave me any lines to say."

"Why not?" Megan asked.

"Because my parents didn't want me to be an

actor and thought if I never got any lines, I wouldn't want to be."

The girls stared at him, but the waitress brought over their chili before they could ask him any more about his parents. They watched as he opened up several packets of crackers and crumbled them up in his hand, sprinkling the pieces over the top of his chili. Then they each did the same. Sara picked up her hot dog. The bun was stale.

"Do you really hit the bad guys?" Megan asked, her mouth full of chili.

He shook his head.

"Do they really hit you?"

"Nope. It's just pretend. All of it."

"Oh."

They ate in silence for a while, then Megan looked over at him. "Do you have any kids of your own?"

"Not yet."

What did that mean? Sara wondered. Did he have a pregnant wife? A pregnant girlfriend?

"If you wanted to, could you really beat up the bad guys?"

Wait a minute, girls, Sara thought. She wanted to go back to the kids he didn't have yet, but didn't know how to get there. After her earlier rudeness, she didn't feel a part of the conversation. She would have liked to interrupt with her own questions, but thought she had already said too much. She took another bite of her tasteless hot dog and kept quiet.

"Where do you live?" Kari asked.

"In a house."

The girls laughed. "That's what our Uncle Joey says," Megan said. She scraped out the last of her chili. "Do you know Mary Lou Lindstrum?"

Mike shook his head, looking puzzled. "Should I?"

"She's in the sixth grade at our school," Kari told

him. "She says she's going to marry you when she grows up."

"Oh, yeah?" Mike looked over at Sara, a twinkle in his eye. "Have you seen her? Is she worth waiting for?"

Sara relaxed. His gaze suddenly made her feel light-headed and lighthearted. "If you don't wait for her, you'd better eat plenty of your magic chili to make you stronger."

He pretended to be worried. "Uh-oh. She's tough, is she?"

Kari nodded. "She gave Willie Newman a black eye last summer."

"Sounds bad."

Sara laughed. "But surely no match for a superhero like yourself. If you can take care of the Dark Avenger, you can take care of Mary Lou."

"But Captain Wonder can't hit girls, Mom," Megan pointed out. "I think he'd better hide."

"I think all he has to do is smile at her and she'll be his obedient slave."

"What's that?" Megan asked suspiciously.

Mike smiled across the table at Sara. His eyes held a hint of amusement, but also gleamed with a promise she did not understand. That same web of intimacy seemed to surround them. "Is that all it takes?" he asked softly.

She found his flirtatious manner more astonishing than flattering. She was a thirty-year-old schoolteacher, the divorced mother of two. He was a TV star, a sex symbol chased by thousands of women. Why would he want to flirt with her? She was not beautiful or sexy or special. Hardly a conquest to boast of.

She didn't like to think he was laughing at her or making sport at her expense, and she was glad when the waitress came to offer dessert. The girls asked for chocolate cake, just as Mike did, and Sara ordered a strawberry sundae. There was nothing like a lot of calories to put her mind back in order.

Sensing their evening was drawing to a close, the girls began to shower Mike with questions about the show and his work. Sara felt relieved rather than annoyed at being allowed to eat her ice cream in peace. Suddenly it felt safer not to have Mike's attention focused on her. He was an actor who used his charm and great looks to his advantage. That was why he was a star—he knew how to attract women and make them feel special. It was his job, but it would be all too easy for her to forget that and fall into the trap of his eyes.

"It was a nice evening."

Sara nodded, then realized Mike would not have been able to see her answer. "Yes, it was." She finished hooking up the camper's water connection and adjusted the flashlight he was holding for her.

"I'm sorry about the money," he went on.

"No problem."

"When I invited you out to dinner, I really did mean to pay. I just forgot I didn't have my wallet. I guess I'm used to people just putting it on my bill."

He moved the flashlight as he spoke and she patiently moved it back again. Actually, she had been glad it had happened that way at dinner. It put them on a more equal footing, where she was less uncomfortable. "It didn't cost that much and was certainly worth all the boasting the girls will be able to do now."

He was silent for a moment. "They're really nice kids."

"Thank you," she said quietly. Had he meant to exclude her? she wondered. Probably, for she hadn't been a particularly scintillating companion. She had been rude and ungracious and then awkward as a thirteen-year-old when he had tried to flirt with her. Oh, well, she'd never thought she could mesmerize a Hollywood star. She hadn't even been able to mesmerize Tom.

She hooked up the electrical connection and wiped her hands on her jeans. "Want that cup of coffee now?"

She led him into the camper and poured two cups of coffee while he sat down at the small dinette table. The girls came scampering over in their pajamas. Megan climbed onto the seat next to Mike; Kari sat across from him, next to Sara.

"How are you going to get back home?" Kari asked.

"Home's in Los Angeles. I was just staying at the hotel back in the park. After I finish this coffee, I'm going to call a friend of mine named Norm and have him come get me."

"We could take you back," Megan offered. "Mommy wouldn't mind, would you?"

"Yes, I would," Sara scolded lightly. "It's already way past your bedtime. Now, say good night and get into bed."

The girls looked crestfallen, but climbed to their feet. "Good night, Mike."

"Hey, don't I get to tuck my buddies into bed?" he asked.

"Will you tell us a story?" Kari asked quickly.

Mike flashed a quick look at Sara. She forced back the spurt of jealousy and nodded. She had been tucking them in for eight years. She could give up one night.

The girls climbed into the double bed in the back of the camper, letting Mike pull the covers up over them. Sara watched from the dinette area, conscious suddenly of how small the camper was. When she had rented it, she had thought it was spacious and roomy. But that had been with her and two eight-year-olds in mind. One six-foot-tall superhero tended to take up a fair amount of space.

She shook her head and forced her attention

from Mike's body onto his bedtime story. It was obvious he hadn't told too many of them, but the girls looked enthralled with his disjointed ramblings about an upcoming *Captain Wonder* episode. They also looked wide awake.

"I think it's time you girls called it a night," she said gently.

Megan nodded and got to her knees. She put her arms around Mike's neck and hugged him. "G'night, Captain Wonder."

He reached over and hugged her back, then hugged Kari. When they were both lying down, he kissed each of them on her forehead. "Thanks for saving my life, buddies."

Sara squeezed by him in the narrow hallway and kissed the girls good night also, then turned off the overhead light. The camper seemed dark with only the light above the table, and Mike's presence became even more threatening to her peace of mind.

Standing at the table, he finished his coffee, then walked to the door. She followed him outside. The ground was covered with a patchwork of lights coming through the windows of the other campers, and the air was filled with the sounds of talking and laughter. Yet, as they stood at the door of her camper, she felt as if they were completely alone. The uncomfortable feeling returned.

"Well, it was fun," she said, feeling stupid.

"Yes, quite a break from my regular routine."

Did that mean he'd been bored? she thought. "I really am sorry about snapping at the waitress like that. It . . . it was really dumb."

She saw him shrug. "I guess I'd better give Norm a call before he goes to sleep."

"Yeah." She stuck her hands in the pockets of her jeans. How did one say good night to a sex symbol? "Do you have change for the call?"

He laughed. "I can call collect."

"Oh, right. I forgot."

"Well, thanks for the meal." He stuck out his hand.

She stared at it for one endless moment, then took it. "Anytime." She shook his hand briefly, then let it go, taking a step back toward the camper. " 'Bye."

She waved slightly and went inside. By the time she turned around to lock the door, Mike was gone. She took a deep breath and walked over to the table to get the coffee cups.

A handshake! she fumed. The world's greatest sex symbol kisses her daughters good night and then shakes her hand! Boy, if that didn't put her in her place, nothing would. She rinsed out the cups and put them away.

Was she really that undesirable? All right, so she was thirty. There were lots of women who were way over thirty and were still considered gorgeous. Of course, they didn't teach third grade in Kansas City. They were actresses with the time and money to devote to looking good. She frowned and went into the bathroom.

She wasn't all that bad, she decided, staring at herself in the mirror. She had a few strands of gray in her short curly hair, but they weren't really noticeable. And her figure was good. Well, reasonably good. She probably shouldn't have had that ice cream sundae or the Snickers bar, but they wouldn't have shown up on her hips already, would they?

As she undressed, Sara studied herself in the small mirror. She was fine, she decided defiantly. Nice. Pleasant. Unexceptional. Totally ordinary. Her kids were cute, that was why he'd kissed them good night. Probably why he'd invited them to dinner in the first place.

She sighed, unable to avoid the truth as she examined her small breasts, narrow waist, and slightly too large hips: she was not sex symbol bait. There was nothing about her to lure any man into an indiscretion, into nights of unbridled passion. She was too boring.

A shower did not wash away the gloom that enveloped her, although she tried to convince herself that she was happy the way she was. She didn't dare to trust her emotions. She had loved Tom, and look where that had led her. Sure, she had the girls and wouldn't trade them for the world, but her relationship with Tom had been a fiasco. He had never understood her or really cared about anyone but himself, yet she had been willing to entrust her happiness to him. She had been stupid then; was she any wiser now? She didn't know, but she doubted it.

Her life was safe, just the way she wanted it. So she didn't date much; she didn't have the time or the inclination for it. Dating was for kids with overactive hormones and time on their hands. She had neither.

Oh, occasionally she would find herself wishing that things could be different. She'd feel vague longings and wonder what it would be like to be swept away by love, but that didn't happen. Not in real life.

She stepped out of the shower and briskly dried herself. What had she really expected? That Mike Taylor, Captain Wonder, savior of the free world, would find her fascinating? She laughed aloud. What a hit she would have been with her third-graders!

After brushing her teeth, she pulled her night-shirt over her head. Captain Wonder clung to her slightly damp breasts. The only way he ever would, she thought. A knocking penetrated her distracted thoughts, and she pulled open the door. Had one of the girls needed to use the bathroom while she was daydreaming? she wondered.

No, the knocking was at the outside door. She hurried over to it and pulled aside the curtain. Mike was back. She opened the door.

"Something wrong?"

He said nothing for a moment, looking hard at her body. At the picture of himself plastered across her chest, actually. She crossed her arms in embarrassment and he looked at her face.

"I can't reach Norm."

She stared at him. What did he expect, that she'd unhitch the camper and drive him back? That would take more than an hour, round trip, and she was exhausted.

"I really hate to impose," he said hesitantly.

She always was a sucker for the apologetic, and stepped aside to let him enter the camper. Then she closed the door behind him.

"I'm tired and I'm not driving another foot tonight."

Mike just nodded slowly. "Okay."

"There's another bed you can use," she said, walking briskly around him. "You may feel a little cramped, but it's better than the floor." She turned to find him watching her with a strange look on his face. "Or the ground."

He nodded and she turned her attention to the dinette area. She took the pillows off the benches and handed them to Mike, then swung the table down to fill in the space in the middle. She rearranged the pillows across the level platform, then glanced up at him. At his long body. She looked down again at the barely six-foot-long bed.

"You'll never fit here," she said with a sudden realization.

"No, it's fine," he assured her. "I curl up when I sleep."

Even curled up, he'd be too big for the bed. She shook her head. "No, I'll sleep here. You can take my bed." She nodded toward the double-bed-sized platform above the driver's seat. "I don't need that much room."

"I really hate to put you to all this trouble," Mike said.

She just shrugged and handed him some sheets and a blanket. "I don't have an extra pillow."

"That's okay."

He took the stuff from her and walked over to his bed. She busied herself making up her own. When that was done, she didn't know what else to say.

"I was just going to bed," she told him.

He finished making his bed. "I'll use the bathroom, if that's okay."

She shrugged as if his presence were of no concern or interest to her, and climbed into bed. He turned the light on in the bathroom and closed the door.

Oh Lord, what had she done? Her kids were at one end of the room while she and the sexiest man she had ever met in her life were at the other!

Mike came out of the bathroom and walked to his bed. It was chest-high, and the ceiling was too low for him to hoist himself up on the edge.

"You'll have to stand on my bed," she told him, moving her feet aside. Her voice sounded strained, even to her own ears.

He nodded and climbed from her bed into his. "Good night," he said.

"Good night." She reached up and turned off the light then turned over, her face to the wall. She was not behaving like the thirty-year-old she was, she thought. He was a teen hero, and she was definitely not a teenager. She was mature. She was responsible. She was horny. She closed her eyes and lay awake long after the sound of Mike's even breathing filled the room.

Three

Mike lay still in the pale early morning light. Just a few feet below him, Sara lay sleeping. Her hair was mussed and her long lashes seemed dark and thick against her cheeks. Her blanket had fallen to one side during the night, exposing a tantalizing sight to his eyes. The thin Captain Wonder nightshirt was stretched tightly across her breasts.

Megan's remarks about wearing it inside out came to mind, and he wondered what it would be like to be close to her heart, in between that nightshirt and her skin. Desire began to grow as he let his gaze travel further along, down the bare expanse of her slightly bent leg and into the shadowy recesses beneath it.

Sara was different from most of the women he had known. Certainly worlds apart from Sylvia. For one thing, she didn't seem to give a damn whether he was around or not. In fact, she seemed to be more annoyed by his presence than eager for it. Maybe she didn't know how many women threw themselves at him, or maybe she had no idea how much he was worth.

He frowned. Maybe she didn't care.

He continued to gaze down at Sara as she slept, thinking of various pleasant ways he could awaken her. The beds were close and he could climb down into hers without making a sound. Then he could put a hand on her waist and gently kiss the hollow of her neck.

His breath started to quicken and he licked his lips as he looked around the camper. The kids were still asleep. Kids! His desire quickly fled, leaving him limp and drained. Damn. What had he been thinking of?

He turned over, lying on his back and staring up at the close ceiling with a frown. Actually, he had found Sara and her kids surprisingly enjoyable company. The frown relaxed into a half-smile. It was comfortable spending time with them. They didn't seem to want anything from him, and treated him with a matter-of-factness that he had not experienced in a long time. He was going to be sorry to see it end. The restlessness that had been plaguing him for the past months seemed to have vanished here, and Sylvia's ultimatum seemed unimportant.

Sara moved slightly in her sleep and Mike's eyes shifted to her again. The nightshirt had inched up a little further. He wondered what he would do if he were the husband and father here. For one thing, he'd know how soundly the little girls slept.

Desire began inching its way back into his body. He'd like to let his hand slide along the smooth length of her leg and up into the shadows under the nightshirt, he thought. He'd like to feel the softness of her breasts beneath him and kiss her warm mouth. Her skin would be fresh and clean, not cloying with the lingering odors of lotions and creams and cigarette smoke. Her hair would be soft and natural. She was so unlike Sylvia and all the others: fresh and honest and somehow all the more alluring.

What would she do, he wondered, if he climbed down into her bed? Would she smile and roll over onto her back, welcoming him as if it were the natural start to her morning? Was she dreaming of him now, her body warming with desire for his? Might she even be awake, aware of his gaze, yet uncertain how to respond? What would it be like to make love to her? he wondered.

A sound startled him and he found himself staring across the room at two smiling faces. He gave the girls a weak grin and then lay back on the bed, closing his eyes.

Difficult, that's what making love to Sara would be.

The sound of the girls' giggling woke Sara, and she discovered, to her dismay, that she had been providing quite a show for everyone. She glanced furtively up at Mike as she sat up, pulling her nightshirt down. He was lying on his back and appeared to be asleep.

Talk about shows—he was providing one of his own. His chest was bare and the blanket cut across his body just below the waist. She could see his shirt lying on a chair, but she wondered if he had taken anything else off. There certainly was no evidence of clothing on that magnificent torso.

She got to her feet and slowly folded her blanket, her glance straying over his chest. His muscles were hard and well-defined, tempting her to touch them, as did the mat of blond hair. She followed its trail down to the blanket, disappointed that her view was cut off, then angry at herself for her reaction. She picked up her sheet and folded it quickly.

Mike was handsome enough on television, she thought, but lying there in the bed near her he was almost irresistible. She wondered if he made love in real life as magnificently as he did on the screen. There, girls fainted in sheer ecstasy when he touched them. Would he have that effect on her?

That was something she'd never know, she thought as she put her bedding away. He was leaving soon, and the sooner, the better. After putting her finger to her lips to caution the girls to be quiet, she went into the bathroom.

What a night! she mused. Sara frowned at the dark circles under her eyes. She had thought she would never get to sleep, and when she finally did, she'd dreamed of Captain Wonder, Tom, and screaming teenage girls.

She was glad Mike was leaving that morning. She supposed she'd have to give him breakfast first, but there'd be no lingering. He'd be gone, and they'd be on their way to the Indian ruins and then to Lake Mead.

She emerged from the bathroom to find everyone awake and talking. The girls were sitting on her bed, obviously delighted to find their hero still around. Sara smiled as if she were used to parading around in front of strangers in an almost transparent nightshirt, but she was cursing herself for not bringing a robe.

She pulled some clothes from a drawer, rejecting her comfortable terrycloth romper in favor of a pair of navy slacks that fit as if she'd been poured into them. It was supposed to be cool that day, she rationalized, and the slacks would be more appropriate. Her choice, she told herself, had nothing to do with its slimming effect on her figure or the fact that she felt like a purple elephant in the romper.

Sara went back into the bathroom and got dressed, then hurried the girls into their clothes. By the time Mike emerged from his turn in the bathroom, they were seated at the table eating breakfast. He had showered and his hair was wet. His chin was covered with blond stubble, making him look much less the superhero. That didn't mean he looked like any old guy on the street. Sara wished he did. She might not feel so torn about seeing him leave.

"We don't have much of a breakfast usually," she said, her tone apologetic.

He sat down across from her, nodding when she offered him a cup of coffee. "Actually, I'm not much of a breakfast eater myself. I usually just have coffee when I get up and then something midway through the morning."

"Want some Rice Krispies?" Kari offered.

He shook his head. "No, thanks."

Before the girls could take over the conversation again, Sara decided to set things straight for the day. "We're heading out of here after breakfast, so I thought we'd just drop you off at the lodge on the way."

"You don't have to do that. I can call Norm and he can come get me."

Like he had last night? she thought. "It's no trouble, and that way I don't have to worry about you being stranded out here."

He smiled at her. "Always the mother, eh?"

Is that what he thought—that she was mothering him? Then why was she torturing herself in these uncomfortable slacks? Instead of answering, she poured herself another cup of coffee.

"So what's next on your agenda?" he asked.

"Montezuma's Castle and Lake Mead, then across to Los Angeles." She kept her voice crisp and businesslike. She was not affected by the blond hairs on his arms that begged to be touched.

"We're going to Disneyland," Kari told him.

"Hey, no kidding. I don't live very far from there."

"Really?" The girls were enthralled.

"Why don't you come with us then?" Megan asked innocently.

Sara could not believe her ears and stared at Megan in horror. She was going to have to have a talk with her daughter very soon. "You've forgotten that we're not going to be getting to Los Angeles for another couple of days," she reminded her. "I'm sure Mike doesn't want to meander around sightseeing. He probably has some business to take care of in town."

"Nope, not a thing."

She fought the temptation to glare at him. "I thought you were in the middle of shooting next season's episodes."

"I am, but the crew will be tied down here a while longer, so I have the rest of the week off."

Swell, she thought. *Now* what was she supposed to say?

Megan took care of that for her. "Then you can come," she cried happily. "Awesome."

"Now, Meg," Sara said, trying to regain some control.

"You said you wished you had someone to help with the driving," Kari pointed out. She turned quickly to Mike. "You can drive, can't you?"

"Everything from a Wondercopter to a Blast Bike."

"How about a camper?" Sara asked dryly.

"That too." His smile was too personal and intimate. Why did he want to go with them? It didn't make any sense. He wasn't interested in her, and adoring young fans were everywhere.

"And it would be so much safer with Mike along," Megan said persuasively. "Auntie Jane was worried because we were going alone. She'd feel a lot better if she knew Captain Wonder was with us."

"I'm sure she would," Sara said. She got to her feet and began to clear the table. Somehow *safe* was not the word she would have used to describe his presence.

"So can he come?" Kari persisted.

Sara put the cereal back in the cabinet. The sane, sensible part of her wanted to shriek "no!" yet her mouth couldn't quite form the words. But why not? She wasn't attracted to that overgrown comic book hero, was she? Did she actually believe that he might find her desirable? She was probably insane, but she turned to smile at the three of them.

"Sure, he can come if he wants to," she said brightly. Lord help her, she hoped he would.

"Do you know what you're doing?" Norm asked as he handed Mike his suitcase.

"Don't I always?"

Norm gave him a meaningful look, then leaned against the car. "There's got to be a female involved. You are *not* a tourist by nature."

"As a matter of fact," Mike said with a grin, "there're three females involved. A mother and her twin daughters."

"Twins? And their mother? You lucky dog. How old is the mother? That could be like triplets." Norm looked envious.

"The twins are eight years old."

Norm frowned. "What's the mother like, then?"

"Nice." Mike shrugged. "I can't actually explain why I'm going."

"Sounds like you're hot to trot with the mother," Norm pointed out.

Mike glared at him. "It's just a little escape from my routine. They're very nice people. All three of them. They're easy to get along with and I'll have time to think. I've been awfully restless lately. Sylvia thinks marriage is the solution, but I'm not sure. A few days with Sara and her kids will be a good test as to whether or not I'm cut out for domesticity."

Norm shook his head. "It sounds like nothing but trouble."

"There's nothing going on between Sara and me," Mike assured him. He tried not to remember the strength of his physical response as he had watched her sleeping. "Sylvia would trust me in a situation like this, so why can't you?"

"*I'm* not a fool. I'm not sure I can say the same for Sylvia." Norm straightened up and took the car keys out of his pocket. "I packed everything you asked for, but there wasn't any room for common sense. Don't blame me if she strands you in the middle of Death Valley."

"She won't." Mike stepped back from the car and watched Norm pull away. Then he picked up his suitcase and walked back toward the camper. Sara met him halfway.

"Your friend came, I see."

"Bringing money and clean underwear."

"All the essentials."

She didn't seem overjoyed to see him and Mike felt a twinge of guilt at the way he had maneuvered her into issuing the invitation. He wanted to test out domesticity, that was all, he told himself. She had nothing to worry about, and he would make sure she understood it.

"If you've changed your mind about taking me along, I'll understand."

She shook her head. "No, it'll be nice to have some company. I just wanted to talk to you without the girls around first."

"Sure."

She was silent for a moment, as if she did not know how to start. "We lead a very quiet life," she said suddenly. "Certainly nothing like your life in Hollywood."

"No wild parties, is that what you're trying to say?" he said jokingly.

She looked hesitant and he regretted his flippancy. "I'll behave, I promise. No four-letter words except *nice* and *fine*. No picking up wild women and no excesses of any kind."

"You're laughing at me."

He sighed. "No, I'm not. I'm sorry if it came out

that way. All I really want is the peace and quiet you already have."

"Is that what you expect? It's obvious that you've never traveled with two eight-year-olds." She frowned a moment. "Why us? That's what I really want to know. You must have a lot of friends and enough money to go anywhere. Why choose to go on a sight-seeing tour of the Southwest with us?"

Mike stared into space for a long moment, not knowing what to say, no longer knowing what the truth was. It was true that he wondered whether he could adjust to a settled life with a wife and family and thought this would be a good test, but that wasn't really all of it. He just couldn't explain the rest.

Maybe it was the two little girls. They were so cute and unspoiled and fun to be around. He hadn't had much to do with kids before, but Sylvia hoped to change that. He was just getting in a little extra practice, that was all.

He glanced over at Sara and saw the worried look on her face. What did she suspect? he wondered. That he was going to seduce her for pure sport? He did have a certain reputation along those lines. The rumors were spread more because it suited his image than because they were true, but she needed reassurance, not explanations. He put his arm around her shoulder.

"I'll be honest with you, Sara," he said lightly. "I like you." He smiled down at her. The worry on her face was replaced by suspicion. "You and your kids," he added lamely.

She did not reply and the suspicion did not leave her face. He could feel the tension in her shoulders.

"I never had much of a family life as a kid. My parents were always traveling from one movie set to another, and I grew up pretty much alone. You remind me of the sister I always wanted, but never had. I can relax when I'm with you."

She did not reply and Mike couldn't decipher the

look on her face. Maybe he hadn't said it plainly enough.

"It sounds terrible to say, but it seems there's always some woman climbing all over me. It's a relief to be with someone who wants me for my driver's license."

A tight little smile came to her face. Hell, he thought, was he getting through or wasn't he? He didn't know, but they had reached the camper, so there was no more time for discussion. He gave her one last reassuring hug and opened the camper door.

"I'm really looking forward to the next couple of days," he told her enthusiastically.

"That's nice. We are too." She went to the front of the camper and seated herself behind the wheel.

Mike sat down at the dinette table, putting his suitcase on the floor near his feet. Kari climbed into the front seat next to her mother and Megan sprawled in a lounge chair across from him, feeding her doll.

He sighed. There was still tension in the air and he really didn't feel comfortable yet. He had assured Sara in no uncertain terms that he would behave himself. That nothing would happen. Nothing could possibly happen. He turned to stare morosely out the window, suddenly feeling rather dejected.

Four

Sara turned onto the highway, more conscious of
the man behind her than of her driving. She forced
her attention onto the road. So he thought of her
as a sister, did he? Well, that was just fine with
her. Terrific, as a matter of fact. She'd known all
along that he couldn't be attracted to her, and
she'd wondered why he had wanted to come with
them. Now she knew.

It wasn't as if she thought it could be something
else. Sara knew there was nothing special about
her and was glad to know the truth. Relieved, even.
She would find it pretty frightening to have a man
like that interested in her. She could never measure up to the other women he had known and
would just worry herself sick about it. This was a
much better relationship. Much more comfortable.
Why, then, did she want either to start a fight or to
have a good cry?

She shook herself mentally and turned to Kari
with a smile. It was time to start acting like a good
"sister" instead of a reluctant hostess.

"Why don't you go back and show Mike which drawers he can use? Then maybe you can offer to trade places with him. He might be more comfortable sitting up here."

Kari went off and, for a time, Sara could hear the murmur of voices and giggles behind her as the girls helped him settle in. That wasn't so hard, she told herself. And it would only get easier as they went on. She'd just be polite and friendly and everything would go smoothly.

He appeared suddenly, sitting down next to her. She took her eyes off the road for a moment to flash a smile at him. She felt his answering grin down to her toes and concentrated on her driving.

"All settled in?"

"Yes. Thanks for the drawer space. I didn't expect it. I hope you didn't have to crowd your stuff too much."

How did he manage to make his voice so smooth? she marveled. Was it natural or the result of voice lessons?

"No problem," she assured him. Suddenly it seemed too difficult to concentrate on both the road and his conversation. Her body's reaction to him was definitely distracting.

She cleared her throat. "Actually, I brought along some warmer clothes for all of us in case the weather turned cooler. There was no real need to keep them inside the camper. They're just as convenient packed in our suitcases in the outside storage compartment." She carefully passed another car. "In fact, if your case is empty, you might want to put it there too."

"Sounds like a good idea."

Having used up her store of conversational topics, Sara fell silent. It was just as well, she thought. To be a good, safe driver she needed to keep her mind on the road and not on idle chatter.

Her hands tightened on the wheel as she sensed Mike's eyes on her. He wasn't watching her, she scolded herself. He probably was just trying to familiarize himself with the camper's controls in case she wanted him to drive.

"Ever drive something like this before?" she asked.

"What?" He sounded startled. "Oh, you mean the camper. No, I haven't." He leaned a little closer. "What is it? Automatic transmission?"

"Yes, and power steering. It's just heavier than a car, that's all." If he hadn't been checking out the camper, why had he been looking her way?

"Want to play auto bingo, Mike?" Kari asked.

He turned in his seat, his legs almost brushing Sara's thigh. Her breath caught in her throat and a jolt of awareness raced through her.

"What's auto bingo?" he asked.

"It's a game the kids play to pass the time while we're driving," Sara told him. Her voice sounded only slightly strained. "It's not hard and they enjoy it."

"Well, if you really think I can handle it, I'll give it a try," he teased.

Megan gave him a card and a crayon. "You have to look for all the things on the card," she told him. "When you see one, call it out so no one else can get it. Then you cross it out on your card."

"And no fair using your special Wonder powers," Kari warned him.

"Okay," he agreed with a laugh. "Human powers only."

"Cross your heart?" both girls chorused.

Mike promised, and settled back in his seat to study his card while Sara glanced over to study him. He certainly didn't look like he needed any special powers to do anything. He looked pretty wonderful just as he was, she thought breathlessly. A look, a touch, the trace of a smile, would be more than enough to make her do his bidding.

"How am I going to find a lake in the middle of the desert?" he asked plaintively.

The girls giggled.

Sara awoke from her meandering thoughts. "Did they give you that card? That's not exactly fair, girls."

"All the cards that are left have lakes on them, Mom," Kari pointed out.

"He picked last," Megan added.

"It doesn't matter," Mike assured her. "It's probably fairer to give me a harder one. Evens out the odds."

"Sure," Sara said, keeping her eyes on the road ahead. She had to watch herself and remember his little "sister" speech. They'd just have some light-hearted family-type fun. That was all she wanted anyway.

"Gas station," Megan called out.

"Airplane," Kari said.

Mike looked around him quickly, then down at his card. "Do I need them too?"

"It's too late," Megan told him. "We already got those. You have to find a different gas station and airplane." She paused, then called out, "Bus."

Mike sighed and studied his card. "Cat. Picnic table. Cement truck. Who made these stupid cards anyway?"

"I did," Sara said with a smile. It wasn't so hard to relax around him, she decided. All she had to do was concentrate on his personality, and not on his body.

She could laugh and joke with him and not even notice how gorgeous he was. The muscular legs that she could see out of the corner of her eye had no effect at all on her. Well, almost no effect. She did have to admit that her body had a slight tendency to tingle with awareness of him, but she was sure that would lessen with time. She'd get used to his presence and see him as the brother he wanted to be. She turned off the road into a gas station.

"Gas station," Mike cried. Sara thought the smile he flashed at the girls was a bit triumphant.

"Very good," she told him, and turned off the motor. "At least you won't go down without a fight."

"Hey, I'm on a roll now."

"Sure," she agreed, and smiled at him.

He smiled back, but the look in his eyes startled her. It was soft and caring, and seemed to imply a bond between them, as if they were sharing not just a joke, but the secrets of their souls. She felt as if his eyes were piercing through the defenses she had carefully built over the years, and it frightened her.

She turned with relief to the attendant who had come to her window. "Fill it up," she told him, and then opened her door. "I'm going to stretch my legs," she called back to Mike and the girls, not daring to meet his eyes again.

What in the world was she doing? she asked herself. Did she really think she could share a twenty-three-foot trailer with the sexiest man in the world and not be affected? He was an actor. He knew how to play on people's emotions, but that didn't mean that *his* were involved. She couldn't let herself forget that. She could enjoy their time together, but she must not let things get out of control. She and the girls made up the family. Mike was a pleasant guest who would be gone in a few days, with no regrets on anybody's part.

She took a deep breath and climbed back into the camper as the attendant returned. She handed him her credit card.

"Why don't you let me take care of the gas for the rest of the trip?" Mike asked.

She took the form from the man and signed it, then entered the mileage and cost in a small spiral notebook she took from the glove compartment. "No, thank you," she said smoothly. They were not in need of handouts, and she didn't want to feel beholden to him. It would be harder to keep her distance then.

"I just want to share the expenses," he protested lightly.

She knew that he was looking at her, but she didn't turn her head. Those eyes of his were dangerous and would blind her to the realities of her life. "The expenses have all been budgeted for," she said, and turned on the motor. "And you're our guest."

"But—"

"Girls," Sara broke in firmly, "we should be at Montezuma's Castle in about fifteen minutes. Better put away your game and use the bathroom if you need to."

Mike and the girls waited as Sara locked up the camper. The morning had been the pits, Mike thought. But why? He'd had the peace and quiet he had been hoping for. No screaming fans had followed his every move, and Sara and the girls were treating him like a regular guy. Why had it been so unsatisfying?

"Come on, Mike," Kari called to him.

He shook free of his thoughts to find that Sara and the girls were already halfway across the parking lot. He started after them.

"Mike's being pokey, Mommy," Megan said.

"He's a big man," Sara assured her. "He won't get lost."

If he was such a big man, he wanted to know, why was she treating him like one of the kids? Maybe that was the problem. He wasn't used to that kind of reaction from the women around him. Well, if she wanted another kid, that's what he'd give her, he decided. He started running forward in short, choppy steps.

"Mommy, Mommy," he cried in a little boy's voice. "Please don't leave me, Mommy."

The two girls giggled as Sara kept them walking

through the entrance to the site. The sidewalk was narrow and Mike was forced to walk behind them.

"I'll be good," he whined.

Sara said something, but he couldn't make out the words.

"What?" he asked.

"She said 'you'd better be,' " Kari told him.

"Kari," Sara hissed, but the girls just laughed. They walked through the visitors' center, then down the path to the ruins.

Not overly interested in ancient Cliff Dwellers, Mike found himself watching Sara as she gave the girls a lesson in Indian history. She was really beautiful, he realized, and he wondered why he hadn't noticed it before. She didn't need any make-up to make her eyes sparkle, or designer clothes to make her body seem soft and inviting.

Maybe it was the love that radiated from her. It was so obvious that she treasured the girls. He thought about what it would be like to be so wanted, to be so secure in someone's love. As they moved on down the path to another ruin, he followed along.

He had never had that kind of relationship with his parents, and, although Sylvia claimed she loved him, he had never seen that look in her eyes. He doubted that it had ever appeared in his either. Was Sara's kind of love unique, or had he just not been lucky enough to find it yet? he mused. What would it be like to be included in the warm circle of her love? Would her body be as soft and giving as her eyes promised?

Sara and the girls climbed up some narrow stairs to peer into the remains of one of the cliff dwellings, and Mike dutifully trailed behind. There was something about Sara that was so intriguing. How could he make her equally interested in him?

When the last of the ruins had been explored, they went to view the diorama. Then there were innumerable pictures to take—pictures of Sara and the girls, of him and the girls, of each girl with Sara, and of each girl with him. One helpful old lady stopped by and offered to take a picture of all of them.

"No, but thank you anyway," Sara said quickly.

"Why not?" Mike asked, and passed Sara's camera to the woman.

He went over and put his arm around Sara's shoulders as the girls stood in front of them. Sara's body next to his felt good and he pulled her a little closer. She glared at him slightly, but he just smiled back innocently.

She smelled as clean and fresh as he had expected, with just a hint of perfume. He ran his hand over her shoulder and down the bare skin of her arm. He could feel the warmth of the sun lingering, hinting at an even greater warmth inside. His grazing touch became slower, more of a caress, as an answering need awoke in him.

"Smile now."

He turned toward the camera, almost having forgotten their volunteer photographer. Then he smiled broadly, but his fingers continued their gentle play, no longer moving much, just pressing against Sara's arm for the contact he felt he needed somehow. A slight quiver went through her and he bit back a smile. Maybe now she'd remember he wasn't one of her kids.

"Such a lovely family," the woman said with a sigh as she snapped one last picture and handed the camera back.

"Thank you," Mike said. Sara looked confused as he passed her camera back to her, but he just smiled and turned to the girls. "Anybody besides me hungry? I'll buy."

"Lunch is back in the refrigerator in the camper," Sara said quickly. "No sense in letting it spoil."

Mike opened his mouth to protest, but everyone had turned away before he managed to get any words out. She had done it again, he realized as he followed along behind Sara and the girls. She had made him one of the kids again. But why? He had sensed she felt the same attraction he had when he'd held her close to him for the pictures. Why had she backed away? Had he misread her reaction?

Well, if she wasn't interested in him, then he wasn't interested in her, he told himself as they went back to the trailer. He wasn't so egotistical that he needed every woman around him to fall at his feet. He watched in brooding silence as Sara and the girls got out sandwich fixings—bologna, cheese, mustard, and tomatoes.

"Just help yourself, Mike," Sara said as she and the girls made their own sandwiches.

He waited until they were done, then moved in to make his. He was actually enjoying this little vacation for the new experiences it presented, like making his own sandwich. Usually he just ate out, or had his houseboy cook for him. He put two pieces of bread onto a paper plate, then piled a few pieces of bologna on them. He was determined to have a good time, even if Sara wanted to play earth mother. It didn't matter to him.

"Mom," Megan announced, "Mike took three pieces of meat."

"That's okay," Sara replied.

"But you said we could only take one," Megan protested.

"That's because you wouldn't eat your bread if I let you take more," Sara replied. "Besides, Mike is a big man."

"For sure," Mike said jovially, glad that she had noticed at least that much. "And Captain Wonder needs three times as much food energy as anybody else," he told the girls.

Two pairs of green eyes stared coolly at him. Mike toyed with one of the pieces of meat, wondering if he should put it back. He didn't like bologna all that much anyway, and he didn't want everybody mad at him.

"Once you touch it, you gotta take it," Kari told him quietly but firmly.

Mike frowned but put the meat down on the bread. They were all treating him like a little kid, he fumed. He grabbed the plastic mustard container and squeezed it over his bread. All he got was a rude noise. The girls laughed hysterically.

"You have to shake it down," Sara explained. With a big smile on her face, she took the bottle from him and shook it. The mustard came out evenly.

"Thank you, Mommy," he said politely. Damn, he thought. It did matter. For some unspoken reason, he didn't want her to mother him. He wanted to feel her hands on him, wanted her lips to taste his. He wanted to lie next to her and discover the passions that lay hidden beneath her demure exterior.

"We have cherry fruit drink," she told him. "Is that all right?"

"Fine." He'd find a way to make her as aware of him as he was of her, he decided. After all, couldn't Captain Wonder do everything?

By late afternoon Mike was getting discouraged. He was no closer to solving his problem with Sara than he had been at lunchtime. How in the world could he make an impression on her when they were trapped in a trailer with two kids, driving through the desert?

If he tried to keep the kids occupied, she thought he was one of them. He could hardly send her flowers or candy, yet when he'd offered to pay some of the expenses, she had flatly refused. He thought he had gotten somewhere when she had accepted his offer to drive for a while, but then she had announced that she and the girls were going to take a nap. She wasn't even going to sit next to him to admire his skill. He was getting nowhere fast.

Hearing the patter of little bare feet coming toward him, Mike glanced up from his driving. Kari sat down next to him.

"Hi, Sleeping Beauty. Megan and your mother still asleep?"

"Yeah."

Out of the corner of his eye he saw her yawn, then stare out the window. Soon he heard the sound of another pair of bare feet approaching.

"My turn for the front seat," Megan announced.

"I just got here," Kari answered, determined to stay put.

"Why don't you ladies share the seat? It's big enough." He was surprised at the firmness in his voice, but it seemed to work, for the two girls quietly divided the seat between them. Maybe he ought to try the firm approach with Sara, he mused.

"Your mother still asleep?"

"Uh-huh," Megan said with a yawn.

"Is she snoring?" Kari asked her.

"Ladies don't snore," Mike said.

"Mommies do."

"Yeah," Megan said. "They go like this." She threw her head back, hung her mouth open, and made a loud noise. Both girls giggled.

Mike couldn't help smiling, but felt a need to defend Sara. "I can't hear her."

"She's quiet now," Megan told him.

"Yeah," Kari chimed in. "It's 'cause you're here. You're a guest and we got to be ladies." They looked down their noses at each other primly.

"I just don't know about you girls," Mike said, shaking his head with a laugh.

"But we know about you," Kari replied.

"Yeah, all about you."

Point, counterpoint. Mike decided not to ask just what they knew about him and they rode for a while in silence as he looked for a way to reopen the conversation. After all, they were the key to understanding Sara. No use letting the opportunity go to waste. Finally he asked, "You girls go on vacation like this every summer?"

"Nope, this is the first time that the budget book said we could go."

"Mommy wasn't sure what the budget book would say 'cause we bought the house last year."

"The house is real nice, though, and we have a room of our own."

"Ladies," Mike said firmly. Two pairs of green eyes stared at him. "I'm confused."

They exchanged quick looks and then Kari started speaking very slowly. "Last year we bought a house. Before that, we lived in an apartment and we all slept in one room. Now Mommy has her room and we have ours."

"And Mommy has a den."

"Not the kind bears sleep in. It's just a little room for her books and stuff."

He chanced a brief glance at them, his lips twitching slightly. "You girls write your own lines?"

They stared at him for a moment. "If we have a ruler," Kari said finally.

He blinked rapidly at the road and decided not to explain. "What I was really wondering about was the budget book," he said quietly. "I've never seen one before."

"I'll get it," Megan offered.

"No, that's okay," Mike said quickly. "Just tell me about it."

"You write numbers in it and it tells you how much you can buy."

"Oh."

"And when you can buy it."

"Yeah, it said if we wanted to go on this trip, we couldn't buy hot lunch in school all year."

"And Mommy couldn't buy any new clothes until next Christmas."

"Grandma bought her a coat."

"That doesn't count. Grandma uses a different budget book." Kari looked directly at him. "Now do you know what a budget book is?"

Mike nodded. He certainly did now. It was having to count every penny twice, that's what it was. And if that wasn't enough, he had crowded himself in with them. No wonder Sara saw him as another kid. He had been acting like one, hanging around for treats with no thought of the cost. If he wanted her to see him as a man, he'd better start acting like one, he decided.

"You guys see your father much?" He wondered why the question was suddenly so important to him.

"Nope. Not since last July."

"Yeah, he gave us a nerf check for Christmas," Megan said.

"It wasn't nerf," Kari corrected. "It was rubber."

"Nerf. Rubber. It's the same thing," Megan insisted.

"No, it's not," Kari argued.

"They both bounce," Mike said quietly.

The twins looked at him.

"That's what Mommy said."

"She threw it out before we could see it bounce though."

So their father was a real nice guy who didn't help with their expenses. Was *he* any better? Mike didn't say anything, but he was beginning to get an idea of the kind of life Sara lived and he was angry. Mostly at himself. Why hadn't he seen how hard it was for her? Instead of moping around wondering why she wasn't falling into his arms, why hadn't he shown her that she could lean on him? Well, all those hard times were going to change. On this trip, she was going to go first class.

"Isn't there anyone to help your mother?" Mike asked. "You know, like your grandfather?"

"Grandpa's dead."

"Besides, Mommy says a person shouldn't be beholden."

"Beholden?"

"That's what we say in Missouri. It means you owe somebody something, and Mommy says you should always pay your own way."

Swell, he thought. A poor but proud little lady. Well, it would make things difficult, but not impossible. No problem at all for Captain Wonder. He'd just have to keep his eyes open for the right opportunity.

After a long period of silence Mike said, "Maybe you'd better see if your mother is awake. We're going to be at Lake Mead soon."

"She's not," they both said together.

"How do you know?"

"She bumps around a lot when she gets up," Kari replied.

"Yeah," Megan laughed. "And she makes groany noises."

"I heard that," a voice called from the back of the camper.

The girls fell back into the seat, smothering their laughter behind their hands.

Mike looked into the rearview mirror and watched Sara pull herself out of bed. Her hair was tousled and her eyes were half-closed, making her look incredibly sexy. He would have liked to park the damn trailer and take her back to bed, but two giggling little bodies next to him were reminders of the impossibility of that. How did couples with large families manage to get the privacy to make love?

Sara carefully padded toward the front and sat in the seat behind the girls. They peeked out at her, still giggling.

"You two keep that up and I'll tickle you to death," Sara threatened.

The giggles continued.

From the corner of his eye, Mike saw Sara force a fierce scowl onto her face, but her eyes were swollen with sleep and her face was flushed. She still looked desirable, but now it was combined with such an appealing vulnerability that he was seized by an irresistible urge to grab her and hold her close to him. He wanted to take care of her and protect her. He wanted to make love to her and let only wonderful things touch her life. Instead, he clutched the steering wheel tightly and stared straight ahead.

After a long silence, during which he fought to get his emotions under control, Mike said, "How about I spring for dinner tonight? This time, I've got money."

"I've already bought some hot dogs and beans," Sara replied quickly.

"They'll keep, won't they?"

"I don't want to take a chance," she told him firmly. "Besides, we shouldn't get into the habit of eating out."

There was an air of finality in her voice. She was so tough, but he had seen that vulnerability peeking through and knew she could use his help. He'd just have to be a little clever. It wouldn't be any problem. Pick up a check here. Buy the girls a gift there. No problem.

He smiled happily. Sara was going to have one terrific vacation without ever being aware of what was happening.

"Dinner's ready," Sara announced.

"Ah, a fiendish plot," Mike called out from the double bed where he and the girls had been playing a card game. "I was finally winning and it just happens to be dinnertime."

"You weren't winning," Megan argued. "I had less cards left than you."

"I was still going to win." He came over to the table, a girl holding on to each hand. "Looks good."

Sara smiled at him weakly, envying the girls' easy manner with him. They were so natural and relaxed, while all she could think of was how gorgeous he was and how many women would pay to trade places with her right now. And what was she doing to win his interest? Making him hot dogs and beans. She sat down with a sigh, wondering if there were any *femme fatale* classes at her local YMCA.

Kari passed the plate of hot dogs around. Each of the girls took one and she noticed that Mike looked around carefully before he took any. "I made two for you," Sara told him, wishing their budget ran to filet mignon and wine. "But there are more in the refrigerator if you want them."

"No, this is fine." Mike took his food and passed the plate to her. He opened the catsup bottle for Megan, then carefully shook the mustard before squeezing it on his hot dogs. He seemed to be enjoying himself, Sara thought, relieved. Maybe he didn't mind the meager meal.

"Have any pickle relish?" he asked.

Sara's heart sank. "No."

"Mommy bought some once but it got moldy 'cause nobody ate it," Megan told him. "She won't buy it anymore."

"Meg!" Sara said. "I certainly would have bought some if I had known Mike wanted it." She didn't want him to feel unwelcome. Lord knows she would have bought a gallon of pickle relish if she'd thought it would help him enjoy their company more.

Megan took a huge bite of hot dog and bun, ignoring her mother's words. "Is it Captain Wonder food?"

"No." Mike shook his head and reached for the

catsup. "Actually, it's something the Dark Avenger tricks me into eating. Good thing you don't have any. It steals my strength."

"Maybe yours was moldy too," Kari said.

Mike nodded. "Might have been. I'll be more careful in the future."

Sara smiled, but somehow she couldn't join in their joking. She was so conscious of Mike that the trailer could have been floating out to the middle of the lake and she probably wouldn't have noticed. She stole a glance at his hands gripping his cup and wondered how they'd feel on her body. She was even jealous of the napkin that brushed his lips, as she longed to do.

He shifted his position slightly so that his leg almost touched hers, and she was suddenly conscious of the heat radiating from him. Heat that matched her own in intensity. She tried to convince herself that the look in his eyes as he gazed across the table at her was merely fond, but she suspected she was fooling no one, not even herself.

"What's for dessert?" Kari asked.

Sara glanced around. Everyone was done but she. "Baths," she announced, and quickly finished the rest of her hot dog.

The girls groaned, but they carefully cleared the table, then trooped back to the double bed and started to change their clothes.

"I'm going first," Megan shouted, and got her pajamas from under the pillow. Kari didn't argue, so her twin went into the bathroom.

"Want some more coffee?" Sara asked Mike.

"I can get it."

She shook her head and got to her feet. "I have to check her bath water anyway." She poured them both some more coffee, then went into the bathroom, relieved to escape Mike's presence for a moment. Maybe her racing heart would have a chance to slow down a bit. She frowned at the inch of cold water Megan had put in the tub. "I think you could use a bit more."

"Mom!"

Sara ran the water until she was satisfied. "I'm sure Captain Wonder takes a good bath," she said pointedly.

Megan did not look impressed, but climbed into the tub.

When Sara returned to the table, she found that Mike had finished clearing it. "You didn't have to do that."

"There wasn't all that much to do," he said. "How about if I wash the dishes and you dry? Our coffee's still too hot to drink."

"Mike, you're a guest," she protested. And making him work wasn't going to help his opinion of her, Sara thought.

He looked almost impatient with her. "Then I'll dry."

She just shook her head and began to run water into the tiny sink. "You don't have to help, really you don't."

But Mike picked up the dish towel anyway. She should have insisted he put it down, but somehow the words wouldn't come. She liked being close to him too much. Even something ordinary like washing dishes seemed exciting. Their hands might touch occasionally and, in the small galley, it was impossible for her not to brush against him once in a while. Even as the thought crossed her mind, her body met his.

"Sorry," he said with a laugh, and moved aside to put away a plate.

She smiled quickly and concentrated on her washing, wishing he hadn't been quite so eager to get out of her way. That rush of desire as they touched had been rather pleasant. Rather strong too. It surprised her that she could feel such a powerful reaction to someone she barely knew.

Of course, she saw him on television every Sunday night, so he wasn't exactly a stranger—not that she'd felt this desperate need to touch him and to feel his arms on her each time she'd watched him cavort about in his Captain Wonder suit. No, this was a new feeling, and one that frightened her as much as it gave her pleasure.

By the time they sat down with their coffee, Sara was feeling somewhat more like herself. Megan had finished her bath and was having a brownie for dessert. Mike took one off the plate too. They looked delicious, but Sara refused to let herself have one. She'd decided that, at least while Mike was here, she wouldn't eat everything in sight.

"Do you take baths, Mike?" Megan asked suddenly.

Sara frowned at her daughter, certain the conversation was going to go in a direction she wouldn't like.

"Yep," Mike answered.

"Does Mommy come in and check if you're doing a good job?"

"Meg!" Sara cried, reddening against her will.

Mike just grinned. "She's welcome to any time."

Megan shook her head. "You'd better be careful, she likes hot water."

"Oh?"

Hot water was definitely what Sara felt she was in, and Mike's obvious enjoyment of her embarrassment only made it worse. "Megan, I think that's enough."

"Well, you told me Captain Wonder takes good baths," she reminded her.

"Finish your brownie." Sara ignored the warm look in Mike's eyes, wishing fervently his glance would move elsewhere.

Kari arrived to have her brownie, distracting Mike into having another. Then it was time to put the girls to bed. She tucked them in and kissed them good night, stepping aside for Mike. He repeated the same ritual, she noticed with a smile.

"Do you kiss Mommy good night too?" Megan asked him.

Sara just stared at her for a moment.

"Should I?" he asked.

"Mommy doesn't kiss men," Kari announced.

"She might," Megan argued. "Julie's mom kisses lots of men."

"Girls, this is not the time for such a discussion," Sara said, finding her voice as she reached over to turn off their light. She refused to allow herself to linger on the thoughts Megan's question had awakened. "Good night."

"Good night."

She and Mike walked back to the table, where he grabbed another brownie. She studied the chocolate crumbs clinging to his lips and longed to lick them away.

"Want to sit outside?" he asked.

"Sure," she agreed quickly. At least the darkness would hide her burning cheeks, the visible evidence of her racy thoughts.

Mike picked up his blanket and walked with Sara to the grassy patch next to the camper. It was dark outside, and quiet. Only the murmur of voices from the other campers broke the peaceful silence. He spread the blanket and stretched out on it while Sara sat primly, Indian-fashion.

"Well, you survived your first day with us," she said quickly, before he could bring up anything the girls had said.

"It was fun. I like your kids."

She didn't know what to say next. She couldn't see his face, but she sensed his nearness. Why had she thought it would be easier out here? The darkness had only attuned her senses to his every movement. She didn't need to see him for her body to react to his presence.

"They sure are enjoying having you along," she said lamely.

"I'm enjoying them," he echoed.

She wondered if he meant it or if he was just being polite. He probably meant it, she decided suddenly. He hadn't spent much time with her, just with the kids, so he really could have had fun. "I thought tomorrow we'd go swimming and maybe do some hiking."

"Sounds fine," he said.

She jumped suddenly when his fingers touched her leg. "We could rent a boat, but I think the girls would get tired of sitting still, and I don't think they swim well enough to water ski." The fingers moved along her skin, brushing it gently, yet leaving a fiery trail in their wake.

"You know best."

Did she? she wondered. If those fingers didn't stop their gentle, rhythmic caress, she wouldn't be capable of coherent thought. "We probably ought to go over to see Hoover Dam sometime too."

"If you like."

Like? What she'd like, she thought breathlessly, was for those fingers to stop. No, wait, she really didn't want them to. She wanted them to go on, to move to caressing other parts of her body. She took a deep breath. "So tell me, Mike, what's your girlfriend like?"

The fingers stopped abruptly and Sara didn't know whether to be glad or not. She told herself she was glad and squelched any arguments from her heart.

"How'd you know about Sylvia?" he asked quietly.

"Somehow I couldn't picture you without a girlfriend."

She heard him change position and felt somehow that he had moved away from her. Her body missed him, even though he could not have stirred more than a few inches.

"She's an actress," he said. "I met her when she did a *Captain Wonder* episode. You might remember her, she played an astronaut."

Why did it hurt to hear him talk about another woman? she wondered. "I never paid that much attention to the different shows, I'm afraid."

"That's right." He laughed. "You aren't a Captain Wonder fan."

She wasn't too sure she could say that anymore, and she was grateful for the darkness that hid her blush. "Has she been in anything else?" Sudden, unwelcome images popped into her head. In his bed, his bathtub, his heart . . .

"She was in three episodes of *Dallas* last year and a made-for-TV movie that never got released," he said. "She's no threat to Katharine Hepburn."

His laughter seemed an affront. "You shouldn't talk that way about her," Sara snapped. "Not if you care about her."

Mike was silent for a long time. Long enough for the crickets to grow unbearably loud and for Sara to regret her sharp words. He was already farther away from her than she wanted. She didn't want him to go away completely.

"She's a nice kid," he said finally. "She thinks we ought to get married, but I don't think either one of us is quite ready for that step."

Sara's heart felt lighter, but she did not want to wonder why. "Would she care that you were here with us?"

"No."

Was that a sign of Sylvia's lack of love for Mike or just a sign that Sara was no real threat? "My mother always said that if you weren't sure you wanted to get married, you surely didn't."

"I think she's right."

There was a laugh in his voice, but Sara didn't know what he found so funny. Did he sense the fear in her heart when she spoke of this girlfriend? Why was it there, anyway? She didn't want to care what he did, but the girls would. They wouldn't want him to be unhappy.

Sara decided·it was time to get away from him.

She wasn't thinking rationally anymore. "I think I'd better check on the girls. Then I'm going to bed. It's been a long day." She rose to her feet.

He stood up and folded the blanket. "I hope you sleep well tonight. I promise, you'll be safe. You shouldn't ever stay awake when Captain Wonder's around. You should sleep better knowing he's there watching over you."

"Right." She laughed, knowing how ridiculous the idea was.

"I detect disbelief. Just wait until the Dark Avenger darkens your door. Then you'll be glad I'm around."

"Definitely."

They climbed inside the camper and saw that the girls were quiet. Mike took another brownie.

"I think I'll take a bath and then turn in," Sara murmured.

"Want me to check your water?"

"No, thanks." But her heart was racing as she undressed, and the cool water did little to reduce the fever in her blood. What would Mike think if he were in here with her? Would he find her as attractive as she found him? Would his hands want to explore her body and find ways to bring her pleasure?

There was no way he could know her thoughts, but Sara somehow found it hard to meet his eyes when she left the bathroom. She felt relieved when he went in to bathe, grateful for the added time to collect her thoughts. She put the brownies away, fixed her bed, and settled in comfortably.

The small light she left on over Mike's bed lit the room with a comfortable, secure glow. She closed her eyes and felt herself relaxing, sinking into a peaceful doze. But her eyes flew open when she felt someone sit on the edge of her bed. It was Mike.

"I didn't want you to feel left out," he said softly, and leaned forward. "I realize you don't kiss men, but I thought you might make an exception for Captain Wonder."

His lips brushed hers ever so gently. Then they touched her forehead, one cheek, then the other. Finally, they returned to her lips, clinging to them with sweet promise as a warmth flooded her veins. Her body cried out to him, but she did not move. Only their lips touched, and all too soon that touch was broken.

"Good night," he whispered, then was gone.

She blinked and saw him climb up into his bed. The light went out and the camper was bathed in darkness.

What was that he'd said? she tried to recall. That she should sleep better knowing he was there? But how was she going to do that now?

Five

Sara was standing in her classroom when one of her students burst through the door.

"Captain Wonder's here!" he cried.

Sara felt a rush of excitement. Why was he here? What did he want? She took a step closer to the door and suddenly Stevie Turkle, the terror of the third grade, burst into the room dressed in a Captain Wonder suit. Before Sara had a chance to acknowledge her disappointment, the room was filled with more small, third-grade-sized Captain Wonders, all running around and screaming.

"Stop it and sit down!" she shouted at the children, trying to restore order. "None of you is Captain Wonder!"

Suddenly a tall figure appeared in the doorway. He, too, was wearing the familiar black and red suit and the children ran screaming toward him. "It's Captain Wonder!" they shouted.

It wasn't, though. It was Tom. Couldn't they see the difference? "No, it's not Captain Wonder," she tried to tell them, but the room was too noisy. The laughing children danced around the man, the noise getting louder and louder. "It's not him, it's just Tom," she shrieked, but no one would listen.

Her eyes flew open. It was morning. She stared at the camper ceiling in relief, the quiet of the room contrasting with the noise of her dream. Lord, he was haunting her. She could't even get any peace in her sleep.

"Sara?"

She turned her head to find Mike standing next to her bed. He was wearing only a pair of running shorts, and he had a steaming cup of coffee in his hand. Her body was engulfed by a sudden wave of desire.

"Want some coffee? It's freshly made."

"All right." She watched as he went back to the galley and poured her a cup, trying to will her treacherous senses to behave.

"Milk?"

She nodded and sat up, leaning against the seat back as she pulled her blanket up over her hardened nipples. She might look ridiculous, she thought, but her fool nightshirt seemed practically transparent. Sitting here with the blanket up to her armpits was better than wrapping it completely around her so she could dash to the bathroom and get dressed. And certainly better than letting him see the effect he had on her.

"Here you go."

He handed her a cup, then sat down at the foot of her bed, leaning against the opposite seat back as if it were the most natural thing in the world. She wished she could look as casual, but it had been quite a while since she'd had a half-naked man in her bed. Or any man, for that matter.

"Take your shower already?" she asked, forcing her eyes onto her coffee and away from the slightly damp mat of blond hair on his chest that her fingers ached to touch. She took a sip of her coffee. It was hot and very strong, she noticed. Just the thing to restore her sanity.

"Yes, I've been up for a while. Started the coffee, then showered and shaved. I'm not a lazybones like some people."

"This is my vacation, remember? I get to sleep late occasionally."

He smiled and stretched his legs out in front of him. They were almost touching hers. She wanted both to move closer and to move away, but she did neither. There was a blanket between them, after all. It wasn't as if they were really lying together. Her cheeks grew red as her mind ran through a quick scenario in which they were lying close together. Very close together. She gulped her coffee.

"Actually, I'm glad that you slept well," he said. "You seemed pretty beat last night, but you look a lot better this morning."

Sara knew exactly what she looked like in the morning and was sure that the word *better* did not quite describe it. Her hair would be mussed, but it was too short to look attractive that way. Her eyes would be puffy and her skin pale. Not a tempting sight, she mourned. She was equally sure that Sylvia in the morning presented a far different picture.

She had no idea what the woman looked like, but she could envision her exactly. Long, exquisite hair. Rosy cheeks and gorgeous eyes. She probably applied her makeup in her sleep so that she woke up looking perfect.

"I *feel* better this morning too," she said, not certain whether discussing Sylvia was preferable to listening to her body's yearnings. "I'm all set for a busy day. Are the kids still asleep?"

"If they aren't, they're being suspiciously quiet, and that doesn't seem like them."

"No, it doesn't."

They were silent for a moment, both fiddling

with their coffee cups. Then Mike looked up at her. "You know, I've been thinking a lot about last night."

"You have?" His kiss flew into her mind, and with it, all the conflicting emotions she'd felt at the time. The desire, the confusion, the fear, but mostly the desire. She imagined his lips on other parts of her body. She thought of his hands stirring forgotten embers to life.

"I think you were right when you said that if I had to wonder whether I wanted to marry Sylvia, then I probably didn't."

"Oh?"

"Yes. I'm fond of her, but not overwhelmingly so," he said. "I would think that if I were in love with her, I would be missing her, but I'm not."

She squelched the sudden bubble of happiness that began to rise at his words. "Doesn't exactly sound like love then," she admitted. "Not that I'm any great expert on the subject."

"You probably know more about it than I do, so I'm going to take your word for it. When I get back to Los Angeles, I'm going to tell Sylvia that I'm not going to marry her."

"Will she be upset?" She would be, Sara was sure. If Sylvia thought she had Mike, she would be devastated when he walked away.

"I doubt it. I think she's decided that her career isn't going too well, and getting married and having a family is a graceful way to bow out. She'll probably just try to latch onto some other guy with money."

"If you think that's how she sees you, why have you stayed around this long? Why were you even considering marriage?"

He smiled. "Hey, us guys with money get lonely too, you know. Since I'm sponging off you, you should have figured that out by now."

She wanted to protest his choice of words and tell him that she was only too happy to have him along, but he had gotten to his feet and was staring toward the rear of the camper.

"Howdy, girls," he said. There was some giggling in reply. He turned to Sara. "I think I'll put my shoes on and take a walk. That'll give you all time to get dressed."

"All right. Thank you," Sara said quickly.

He was gone in a moment. She climbed out of the bed she had shared with him in one way, but not in the way she would have liked. The Captain Wonder on her chest was rather wrinkled from the blanket and she tried to shake the wrinkles out, but his face seemed permanently smashed. Well, that's what he got for sticking so obscenely to her chest, she told herself with a half-smile.

"Come on, girls," she called. "Let's get dressed."

They tumbled from the bed. "Can we wear our new T-shirts?" Kari asked.

"Nope." Sara went to her drawer and pulled out shorts and a shirt, suddenly nervous and determined not to let Mike get any closer to her. "I think you should save them for when we get home. You wouldn't want someone to see your shirts and then recognize Mike. He wants to relax, not be pestered for autographs."

"You wear your Captain Wonder shirt," Megan pointed out.

"That's a nightshirt and no one sees me in it."

"Mike does."

"I think Mike knows he's Captain Wonder," Sara said. "Let's just not let the rest of the world know right now."

Kari nodded. "Yeah, let's keep him to ourselves."

Sara smiled. She liked that idea, even if it was only for a few more days. She plugged in her curling iron. No reason she shouldn't look presentable for a change, she decided, even if she was going to do her best to build a wall around her heart.

The day passed all too quickly for Sara. They spent the morning at Hoover Dam, then went back to the camper for lunch. She tried hard to relax around Mike, pretending that he was one of her brothers or cousins, and not the sexy idol of millions. It worked only as long as she couldn't see or hear him, and when he was at least ten feet away. Any closer, even if her back was toward him, and her body burned with desire. She did not need her eyes or ears to tell her he was there.

After lunch they all took a hike through the woods. The girls skipped ahead of Mike and her, occasionally darting off the path to explore things, and showing little interest in the adults' conversation. Although she couldn't quite relax around Mike, Sara realized she could still enjoy his company. He made her laugh more than she had in a long time, though her laughter became rather strained when he suddenly took her hand.

It was a natural thing to do, she told herself. The path was narrow and they were brushing shoulders often. But her heart started to race and she began to have trouble thinking coherently, let alone speaking. Could he feel the tension racing through her? she wondered. Did he suspect the kind of thoughts that had been haunting her?

In spite of her concerns, Sara felt disappointed when they left the narrow path to return to the camper and the reason for holding hands was gone. She tried not to think how empty her hand felt, and just hurried the girls inside to put on their bathing suits.

While Mike changed in the bathroom, she and the girls used the rest of the trailer. She had bought both of the girls brightly colored tank suits just for the trip, but she hadn't bothered with any such extravagance for herself, figuring that her old two-piece suit from her honeymoon was still fine. Now she regretted her frugality. That suit was more than ten years old and looked it. What's more, her stretch marks showed. To cover up her worst faults, Sara thought ruefully, she'd have to stand in water up to her waist. No, up to her chin. Her chest wasn't anything to brag about either.

"Safe to come out?" Mike called from the bathroom.

"Yes." No reason for him to stay in there any longer, she thought. Her looks wouldn't improve in the next five minutes. She had busied herself gathering some towels together when she heard the bathroom door open.

A low whistle pierced the air. "My, my," Mike said softly. "Who's the gorgeous lady that wandered in?"

As the girls giggled in delight, she spun around to find him looking at her with definite approval in his eyes. The blush that covered her body must have looked brighter than a bad case of sunburn.

"Mommy says she doesn't look good in a bathing suit because her baby lines show," Megan told him.

"Baby lines?"

"Stretch marks," Sara explained quickly, wondering when Megan would learn to keep her mouth shut.

"I don't see any," Mike said.

"She's got the towels over them," Kari pointed out.

Her own two daughters were out to get her! "Don't you think we ought to be going?" she asked.

No one paid any attention to her words as Mike walked over and gently pulled the towels from her hands.

"See, there they are," Kari said, touching the marks with her finger.

"What is this? Show and tell?" Sara asked in a mocking tone.

To her delight and dismay, Mike's finger began tracing along the same path as Kari's. "I don't think they're anything to be ashamed of," he said.

She trembled under his gentle touch and did not dare look into his eyes for fear he would see the yearning in hers.

"I can barely see the lines, but just knowing they're there makes you look even better to me," he went on.

His voice was a whisper-soft caress that turned her blood to fire. Her knees were threatening to give way under her and Sara thought there was nothing she'd like better than to sway into his arms.

"See, Mom, we told you they didn't show," Megan said, bringing her back to reality.

Sara took the towels from Mike. "You guys are all just too nice. Thank you for the reassurance." She shooed the girls toward the door, trying hard to ignore Mike's overwhelming presence. "Don't you think we ought to get out there before the sun's all used up?"

"Oh, Mom!" the girls groaned, but hurried out happily.

Mike stayed right behind her. She could feel his eyes on her and wished she had wrapped the towels around her body. But then, he'd said she looked good. Had he really meant it, or was he just being polite? Courtesy didn't demand that he make any comment, she reminded herself. Feeling confused, she locked the trailer door and walked down to the beach at Mike's side.

The beach was marvelous—smooth and clean and almost empty. The water was pleasantly cool and the sun hot. Sara felt herself glowing in the perfection of the setting and under Mike's admiring gaze. She joined him and the girls in the water to play for nearly an hour, then climbed out and lay down on her towel to get a tan. Mike stayed with the girls for a while longer, but then left them playing in the sand to sprawl next to Sara.

"Did they wear you out?" she teased.

"Are you kidding?" he scoffed. "I could have

stayed in the water with them for hours yet." He leaned on his right arm as his left hand reached over to touch her. Ever so gently, he let his fingers trace the stretch marks. Her stomach quivered in delight.

"Ticklish?" he asked.

"Only my stretch marks."

He smiled slowly, his eyes warm and inviting, promising things that her mind might not understand but her heart could. "I guess I'd better find a different place to play, then," he said lightly.

His fingers slid slowly upward, past her waist and up to her breasts. He let one finger wander over the edge of the cup and down over her smooth skin. The heat of the sun was nothing like the fire racing in her blood at his touch. Her hands ached to touch him, too, but something kept holding her back. Maybe it was the girls' laughter floating toward them from down the beach, or maybe it was the beach itself. She wasn't used to being seduced in public.

Mike seemed to sense her hesitation. His caresses stopped. He put one finger to his lips and placed a kiss there, then touched it to her lips.

"Do you know how easy you are to touch?" he said quietly.

Sara stared at him as he lay back and closed his eyes.

"My hands seem to have a will of their own when you're around," he went on. "I promised to try to behave, but I can't promise anymore. Some things are too strong even for Captain Wonder."

What about Mike Taylor? Sara thought with a smile, noticing how often he referred to himself as Captain Wonder. He might think the two were one and the same, but she didn't. She had no doubts that it was the flesh-and-blood Mike Taylor who aroused her so, not the comic book hero. Captain Wonder was good for a laugh, but laughter was not the overriding emotion she felt when Mike was near.

She said nothing, though, and used the chance to gaze at him without his knowledge. The fine blond hair that covered his body was darker from the water, but as she watched, tiny strands dried and curled up. Her gaze traveled over his flat stomach to his white swim trunks. They clung tightly to him, teasing her mind with images of the body they covered. She forced her glance down to his legs, where bits of sand clung. Her fingers itched to brush them off, but she made herself look away. No, it wasn't tights and a cape that turned her on, that was certain. Her eyes focused on the girls, who were working feverishly in the wet sand.

"What are the girls making?" she asked.

"Sand castles," he said simply, and, opening one eye, he studied the results. "They have to have towers," he called out. "More than one. And a moat."

"Slave driver," Sara said, laughing under her breath.

He lay back on his towel and grinned at her. "I have to do something to get a moment alone with their mother." He picked up her hand and brought it slowly to his lips, kissing her palm with exquisite tenderness.

She was at a loss for words, but she let her hand linger in his. His eyes were so soft and caring, she thought, his gaze like a caress. It left her breathless and hungry for the feel of his body along hers. She had never before needed a man the way she needed him, had never even known that desire could run so fiercely through her veins.

"Mike! We're done!" Two happy voices broke the silence.

"Talk about rotten timing," he muttered with a laugh. "Don't go away." His finger touched her cheek; then he was hurrying over to join the girls.

She watched him for a moment, then lay back and relaxed. It was so peaceful here. She was sorry that they were only staying at the lake until tomorrow morning, but there was so much they wanted to see and so little time to see it. They had all been in such a rush to get to Los Angeles and Disneyland. Little did they know they'd find their own Fantasyland along the way and would be almost sorry to reach their destination. It would mean that their vacation was more than half over, and that Mike would be leaving. She was going to miss him once they were on their own again.

Suddenly she became aware that someone was standing over her. She opened her eyes to find Mike towering above her, and next to him were the girls. They were giggling suspiciously.

"I'm afraid it was a tie," Mike told her.

"A tie?"

"Our castles," Megan said quickly, in between giggles. "Mike said they were both so good that he couldn't pick a winner."

"That's wonderful," she said hesitantly. What was there to be suspicious about? Nevertheless, she was.

"So neither of us lost," Kari added.

Sara frowned at them. Something was definitely going on. "That's how it usually works in a tie."

The girls looked at Mike and giggled some more.

"Would someone like to tell me the joke?" Sara asked impatiently.

Mike shook his head. "There's no joke," he said sadly. "It's just the deal that your daughters agreed to." He leaned over and scooped her up into his arms.

"What are you doing?" Sara cried, shocked. Held firmly against his chest, she saw the girls jumping up and down in delight. "What is going on?"

"When you have a contest, somebody has to lose," Mike pointed out. "Your loving daughters decided it had to be you."

A cascade of giggles was the girls' only response.

"Enough is enough," she said sternly. "You can

put me down now." Her body was not to be trusted. She wanted Mike so much that she had to keep reminding herself that he was a sex symbol, the object of desire of thousands of women, and that he would be out of their lives completely in a few days. It wasn't right to need his touch so much, she thought.

"Sorry," he said, smiling down at her. "All I'm doing is obeying orders." He started walking toward the water.

"What orders?" she cried, holding onto him to keep her balance. His skin burned her hands like fire, and a tremor of awareness passed through her. She prayed that he hadn't felt it, but his hold tightened.

"Loser gets dunked," Megan cried happily.

"Dunked!" She was all nice and dry now. She didn't want to get wet again. "Thanks a lot, girls."

"It was the deal, Mom. And you said you're not supposed to go back on a deal."

"But I didn't make this one."

"It was made for you," Mike told her.

His mouth was much too close to hers for her peace of mind and she tried to glare at him. "I don't want to be dunked."

He just smiled as he entered the water. Some of it splashed onto her back and it felt cold.

"Mike!" she shrieked.

The girls squealed with delight at her predicament. "It's okay, Mom," Kari assured her. "Captain Wonder won't let you drown."

Drowning was the least of her worries, Sara thought. And she was more concerned about Mike Taylor than Captain Wonder. "I'll get even with you for this," she muttered.

He didn't look terribly worried and walked further into the water.

"Mike, I mean it." Too much of his skin was against too much of hers. He might be used to this kind of contact, but she wasn't. "I thought Captain Wonder was a gentleman."

"Captain Wonder?" he mocked gently. "Who's he? I don't see any dumb-looking guy in tights around here."

The water was lapping at her feet. "Drop her there," the girls shouted.

"No, it's too shallow," he answered.

"Mike, I don't swim very well," she protested, but he kept on walking. The water splashed her back, swirled around her sides, then went over her stomach. She clung a little tighter to him. How deep was he planning to go?

"Remember you're taller than I am," she said.

His smile was devastating. "Don't you trust me?"

"Come on, Mike," the girls called from where they had stopped in the water. "If you don't drop her there, it won't be any fun."

"Depends on what you consider fun," he murmured.

Sara eyed him uneasily. "And what is your idea of fun?"

"Let's say, deep enough to hide from curious little eyes." As he spoke, his hands let go of her and she sank.

The girls were roaring with laughter when she surfaced, her neatly curled hair now wet and straight, was falling into her eyes. Mike's hands went to her waist to support her.

"Was that so terrible?" he asked.

She pushed her hair back and glared at him. It wasn't fair that he could stand in the water and she couldn't.

"You could have picked shallower water," she said. She tried to swim away from him, but found his hold was too tight.

"Where's the fun in that?" he asked softly.

Although his hands still supported her, Mike put one leg forward so that she could rest against it, but it did not add to her peace of mind to have his leg between hers. The skin of her inner legs felt the strength of his leg muscles. There was no way that she could stand with her head above water, so she didn't even try. Instead, she pressed the soles of her feet against his lower leg, moving them slowly with the rhythm of the water, exploring at least that part of him.

At the same time, Mike's thumbs gently brushed against her breasts and his fingers ran over her lower back. It felt all too good, she mused. She wanted it to go on, but somewhere away from the girls' curiosity. Somewhere where she'd feel free to touch him back. To let her fingers roam over his body, to explore it as slowly as she wanted without even their bathing suits to restrict their movements.

What in the world had come over her? Sara wondered suddenly. Things were moving too fast in a direction she wasn't sure she wanted to take. She knew he was leaving in a few days. Why was she allowing herself to fall under his spell? It was time she returned things to a calmer level.

"Last one back is the Dark Avenger," she called out as she twisted abruptly. At the same time, she skimmed the palm of her hand along the top of the water. A spray of water hit Mike in the face and he let go of her. She did a rather sloppy surface dive and swam away, reaching the girls long before he did.

"I thought you said you couldn't swim," he protested.

"A desire for revenge gave me hidden strength." She laughed and splashed the girls and Mike. "So, you guys are going to plot against me, are you? You'll be sorry."

· The girls laughed and tried to escape, but she chased them and suddenly they were all involved in the fun, laughing and playing until hunger drove them back to the camper for dinner.

"Good night, girls," Sara said firmly, and turned off the light. They had had an exhausting day and she knew they were tired, even if they wouldn't admit it yet. She was certainly ready for bed. She had been very tired after the swimming, but they had taken a long walk after dinner and now she had really had it.

Mike was washing out the coffeepot and he smiled at her yawn. "Someone's sleepy."

"You better believe it." She went over to the table and swung it down, then rearranged the pillows to form her bed, trying to ignore the way Mike had fit right into their lives. She felt as if she had known him forever, as if it was perfectly natural for him to be washing out the coffeepot while she made the bed. And then, of course, to join her in it. She forced herself to make casual conversation. "Those rocks reaching into the lake didn't look that far away when we started hiking there. Do you think somebody moved them while we were walking?"

"Shall I put on my Captain Wonder suit and investigate?"

"Only if you can do it quietly, and without turning on any lights." She made up her bed, then smothered another yawn with her hand. "I don't know about you, but I'm going to bed. If you want to read or something, the light won't bother me. I'm going to be unconscious the second my head hits the pillow."

"No, I think I'm ready for bed too."

His voice had a peculiar tone, but she was afraid to analyze it. It didn't matter what he meant; the girls were providing her with proper chaperonage in case her emotions threatened to overwhelm her good sense. Sara took her nightshirt and the long sweater she was using for a robe and went into the bathroom. A few minutes later she finished cleaning up the kitchen while Mike took his turn in the bathroom. She was just locking the door when he came out, and walked toward her, turning off the light over the stove as he passed it.

"Aha, is this an intruder?" he whispered teasingly as he leaned against the closet.

She was all too aware of being trapped in the tiny alcove formed by the end of her bed, the closet, and the door behind her, and she was glad when he took a step closer, out of the girls' line of vision. Being seduced by a superhero was bad enough without having her daughters witness every flutter of her heart, Sara thought wildly.

"Do you know the password?" he whispered. "I can't let you pass without it."

"Captain Wonder?" she whispered back.

"Wrong," he said with a grin. "Looks like I'll have to investigate further."

Before she had time to take in his words, he had moved even closer and pulled her into his arms. His lips found hers with amazing accuracy as he pulled her body against his. Her sweater-robe provided no protection from his sensual onslaught; neither did her Captain Wonder nightshirt. Her breasts were crushed against his chest, the rough hair teasing them through the thin fabric as his lips devoured hers.

His hands roamed over her back, sliding under the sweater as he drew her ever closer to him. His thin shorts could not hide his need for her, and she felt a thrill go through her, knowing that she had such an effect on him. When his hands began to slide up under the bottom of her nightshirt, she made no protest. She wanted his hands on her just as much as he did.

"Hey, stop taking all the sheet," one of the girls complained sleepily.

It was more effective than a cold shower. They pulled apart immediately without saying a word.

"I don't have it all. You do," the other one replied.

"Girls, get to sleep," Sara said with a sigh. She didn't know whether to be glad of the rescue or not.

Mike leaned over and brushed her lips with his. "Good night," he whispered.

"Good night," she whispered back, and moved silently past him to climb into bed.

She felt his weight slightly as he used the edge of her bed to climb up into his, then the room was silent, lit by the moonlight streaming in through the windows, but peaceful and still.

It had been some day, Sara thought. Besides exhausting her body, she had exhausted her spirit. She had lowered so many of her defenses. She had allowed Mike to get close to her, closer than she had let any man get since her divorce. Why had she done that?

Visions of herself in Mike's arms raced through her mind. She imagined the strength of his embrace and the magic in his lips. What would have happened if the girls had been asleep? Would they have made love, or would she have come to her senses? Unfortunately, she realized, it was her senses that kept responding so strongly to him. They still were, as a matter of fact. She rolled over on her side, sure that sleep was a long way away.

Six

"That was a lot of fun," Mike said warmly.

Sara kept her eyes on the road. "Yes, it was." They had left Lake Mead just after lunch, hours later than she had planned. But the place had been so special, so magical, that she hadn't minded staying a little longer. When Mike and the girls had wanted to swim again in the morning, she had agreed to postpone their departure. They still had plenty of time to get to their campground in Los Angeles before eight P.M. Their reservation was in no danger, even if her heart was, she mused.

"Want to play bingo, Mike?" Kari called to him.

"Sure. I'm getting pretty good at it." He got up, his hand brushing Sara's shoulder in a gentle caress before he went back to get his card and crayon. He repeated the gesture when he returned.

Sara turned to him with a smile. "The girls could have brought you your card."

"The exercise is good for me," he protested as his crayon slipped from his hand. He bent down to pick it up, his fingers somehow managing to linger a moment on Sara's leg.

"Mike, I'm driving," she hissed. "That could be dangerous."

"I know," he murmured, his eyes full of meaning. "This trip has been filled with dangers I hadn't expected."

Sara wanted to ask him what he meant. She wanted to look again into those eyes, to be sure she understood what they were saying. But the speed she was driving at wasn't conducive to romantic discussions; neither was the presence of the girls.

"We're going to miss *Captain Wonder* tonight," Megan announced.

"Hey, you've had Captain Wonder with you every night," Mike teased.

Sara joined in the laughter, but his words troubled her slightly. Who was really traveling with them? Captain Wonder or Mike? Were they two separate people, or had he just been playing a part while in their company?

"It's just a rerun anyway," Sara assured the girls. "The new shows don't start until the middle of next month."

"Around our birthday," Kari said.

"You girls got a birthday coming up?" Mike asked. "How old are you going to be? Thirty-five?"

Kari laughed. "No, nine."

"Want to come to our party?" Megan asked.

"Sure. I like parties."

Had this trip been just a party for him? Sara wondered. Had he merely been amusing himself with them? The farther she drove from the peacefulness of Lake Mead, the more she let depression overtake her. The magic of their days together had blinded her to some hard facts that were now all too clear: he would be leaving them that evening.

She had known it all along and had even reminded herself of the fact occasionally, but she knew now she hadn't really been listening. Her mind had been working on one level, but her emotions were on quite another. The girls seemed to have reality firmer in hand than she had. They were going to miss Mike when he left, but she suspected she was going to be almost devastated. Why had she let her feelings go beyond good sense?

She resolutely took a deep breath and concentrated on the road, the flat desert stretching for miles on either side. She wasn't going to spoil their last afternoon together by constantly reminding herself that it wasn't going to last. This was a vacation and everybody was supposed to have a good time on vacations. She'd known all along that vacations didn't last forever. Sara's mental ramblings stopped as she spotted a gas station and pulled the camper over.

"Oh good, a chance to walk around a little," Mike said.

Sara looked at him with surprise. They hadn't even been on the road for an hour. Well, maybe a man of his size found the camper more confining than she did. A few minutes' stop wouldn't matter, she decided. Mike got out first, then helped each of them down. The sensation of his touch lingered long after he had removed his hand from her arm.

Why was she letting herself react this way? She knew she was just opening herself up to hurt, but she couldn't help it. The more she was with him, the more she longed for his touch. The more she wanted to be in his arms, the more she needed him.

"Fill it up, friend," Mike told the attendant. Sara hadn't even noticed his approach. "And give it a thorough checkup: oil, water, as well as all the different belts."

Sara and the girls watched the attendant put the gas nozzle into the tank.

"Why don't you walk around a bit?" Mike suggested. "I'll take care of this."

"I thought I'd pay first," Sara said. "Then we

could park the camper and all walk around." They had only a few more hours together, and she wanted to spend them with him.

"Oh, Mom, look at all the neat stuff," Kari said, pointing to an open-air souvenir stand next to the gas station.

"Go ahead and look," Mike said, laughing. "I'll tell the attendant he can cut off my hand if you run away without paying."

His smile seemed so special, so much for her alone, that Sara found herself nodding and hurrying after the girls, lost in a private pleasure. She caught up with the girls at a display of Indian costumes.

"Aren't they beautiful, Mommy?" Kari asked.

"They sure are neat," Megan added.

Sara sighed. Her own ridiculous longings for Mike made her even more sympathetic to the girls' longing for treasures beyond their reach.

"They're just too expensive, girls," she said gently. "And they aren't something you'd have much occasion to wear."

"We could wear them on Halloween," Megan pointed out.

Sara shook her head slowly. "We just can't afford to spend that much for a Halloween costume. How about these headbands with feathers?"

They agreed without enthusiasm and replaced the dresses on the rack. Sara knew just how they felt. When someone wanted something so badly, it was almost impossible to count the cost. Look at how badly she wanted Mike, she thought, and at the price she'd have to pay in disappointment when he left. Yet, even knowing that, she would not have done anything differently if she could have.

"Hi, girls. Anything terrific around here?" Mike noticed the girls wistfully touching the Indian dresses.

Startled by his voice, Sara looked up at Mike.

"The camper all ready to go? We'll just pay for these headbands and then we'll be all set too."

"No hurry," Mike said, his hand gently squeezing her arm. "I want to get a newspaper."

Sara paid for the headbands, then she and the girls went over to the station to pay for the gas. She saw that their camper had been moved off to one side and hoped that the attendant wasn't too irritated about waiting for her to come back.

"Sir," she said, "I'd like to pay for my gas."

The man gave her a strange look. "Your husband already paid."

Sara felt her cheeks redden and her body warm, but chose to ignore his mistake. "He wasn't supposed to pay!"

Kari wanted things clear, though. "He's not her husband. He's just riding along with us."

The man glanced from Sara's burning face to the girls, then shrugged. "I really don't care, lady. You're all square and can leave anytime you want." Another customer appeared and he turned away to write up the charge slip.

After hesitating a moment, Sara stalked out, pulling both girls along. Her eyes were filling with angry tears.

"It was nice of Mike to pay, wasn't it, Mommy?" Megan said quietly.

"Yes, it was." Sara spoke through clenched teeth. She had thought the money issue had been settled before. She didn't want his money, and what she *did* want from him she couldn't have.

They got to the camper just as Mike came rushing over with a package. "Hope I didn't make you wait too long," he said brightly.

"I told you I was going to pay for the gas," Sara said without preliminaries.

"Yeah, I know," Mike said with a nod. "But they wanted me to move the camper so I had to pay. You know how pushy those people can get."

Sara felt an immediate rush of guilt for misjudging his motives, and her tone softened. "Well, I'd like to pay you back."

"Sure," he agreed. "I'll look for the receipt. I'm sure I stuck it in one of my pockets." They went inside. "Want me to drive now?"

"No, it's still my turn," Sara said. "You look for the receipt."

But no receipt was forthcoming after they had been back on the road for a while. She looked suspiciously into the rearview mirror. The three of them were playing Old Maid at the dinette table. "Mike, the receipt."

"Oh, yeah." He glanced up at her with a smile. "I'm looking. I don't know where I could have put it."

"Maybe it's in the bag from the souvenir store," Kari suggested.

Mike grinned. "Good idea, Kari. I'd better look there."

She heard the rustle of paper as he opened the bag, then twin squeals of delight. Her eyes jerked back to the mirror.

"I'll be a son of a gun," Mike exclaimed. "They must have given me someone else's bag."

"You got the Indian dresses," Megan said breathlessly.

Sara looked back to see two Indian dresses in Mike's lap. Her eyes narrowed suspiciously.

"Boy, I sure can't wear these," Mike said with a laugh. "I guess you girls will have to take them."

"We can take them back," Sara said quickly. Seeing a turn around up ahead, she moved into the left lane.

"It'd be a waste of time to go back. I threw the receipt away," Mike said.

There was dead silence behind her.

"I don't know what I can do with these dresses if you don't want them," Mike said slowly. "I can't use them myself. I guess I'll just have to throw them away." His voice sounded remarkably like Megan's when she was trying to get her way.

It was quiet, but Sara could feel the tension behind her. She heard a soft sound and could see the girls staring down at the table. He must have put the dresses back in the bag.

"Are you sure you girls don't want them?" he asked casually. "Like I said, *I* can't wear them."

Again there was silence, and Sara gripped the steering wheel so hard, she could feel her shoulder muscles clench. This was no accident, she decided, and neither was his paying for the gas. He was just playing some kind of game. But was it fair to hurt the girls because she and Mike were having a disagreement?

Finally she exhaled slowly. "If they want them, they can have them."

There were screams of delight behind her and a scrambling of little feet. "Can we wear our headbands with our dresses, Mom?"

"Yes," Sara said quietly.

There was a great deal of laughing as they changed into their Indian dresses. Mike came up to sit next to her. He looked terribly pleased with himself.

"Silly of me to throw away the receipt," Mike said. "I'm always doing that. Drives my accountant nuts."

"I imagine you did that with the gas receipt too," she said tightly.

"You know," he said earnestly, "I bet I did."

Sara didn't seem very receptive to his company and, since it was still a while before his turn to drive, Mike decided to take a short nap. He hadn't slept too well the night before. Sara's presence had disturbed him somehow, and she had lingered in his thoughts far later than she should have. Might be just as well if he could get in a few hours of sleep now, he thought.

He rolled over on his side and looked toward the wall, a warm smile covering his face. He had enjoyed surprising the girls with those costumes and taking care of the gas for Sara. He knew that Sara was a little miffed about it, but he suspected that was mostly her pride. Once she cooled down some, he was sure she'd see how nice it was having a man to lean on. And he was surprised at how much fun it was to take care of someone.

There were so many things he'd like to do for them, things that would make them smile and laugh. Sara in particular. How he'd like to keep that little frown of worry from ever appearing on her forehead again. It didn't seem right that someone so gentle and kind and loving should have so many burdens.

She was such a beautiful woman, he reflected, and in so many ways. Twenty, thirty years from now she'd still look great, because her beauty was all through her, not just on the surface.

Of course, her surface was pretty terrific too. He'd had a few chances to check it out over the last couple of days and only wished he'd had more. Those few minutes of contact in the water and their all too brief kisses had only served to whet his appetite. He'd like to have the chance to touch her without a bathing suit hampering his enjoyment and two little girls cooling his ardor.

Suddenly Mike's dreams erupted into a painful need. He wanted to make love to Sara, to feel her body next to his. He wanted to touch her, to hold her, to make her want him the same way he wanted her.

"Are you awake, Mike?" Kari asked from right behind him.

"He can't be asleep already," Megan insisted.

Oh Lord, what timing! he groaned silently. If he

lay still, would they go away? He forced himself to relax, in an effort to make his body behave.

"I think he's just faking," Megan said.

Damn. Why wouldn't his body act in a civilized manner? He had never known this intensity of feeling for any other woman. Why for Sara? he wondered. He rolled onto his stomach.

"Hold him down and I'll tickle him to death."

Mike's eyes flew open and he stared at the wall in front of him. "Hold who down?" he was able to ask. But before his question could be answered, he felt the bed bounce slightly and two little bodies scramble on top of him. Little fingers wiggled into his armpits.

"Hey," he cried.

"What's going on back there, girls?" Sara asked quickly.

"We're just playing with Mike," Kari said sweetly.

He tried to turn his head and look up at her, but she was sitting solidly on his shoulders. He was about to tell her to get off when a giggle warned him. He was almost able to tighten his muscles before a little cannonball with knees bounced on the small of his back.

"Are you girls playing rough?"

"Not real rough, Mommy," Megan answered. Mike was amazed at how sweet the little assassin's voice sounded.

"It's real cramped back here, girls," Mike said, raising his voice slightly. "Someone could get hurt if we fool around."

The girls did not move.

"Girls, get up here, please." Sara's voice was sharp. The girls slowly slid off the bed and trooped back up to the front of the van.

Mike sat up slowly. His body was relaxed, if a bit sore. He swung his feet to the floor. On the edge of the bed lay two pieces of paper which he picked up. They were letters to him from the girls, thanking him for the Indian dresses.

He read them slowly, then looked up to where the girls were sitting. Hell, he was going to be real sorry to see this trip end. He had enjoyed the girls more than he had thought possible, and he wanted even more to get to know Sara better. He felt so drawn to her and hated just to let them all walk out of his life. If only there was a way to make it last longer, he thought.

He rose, walked slowly to the jump seat across from the dinette table, and sat down. "Want me to drive?"

"No, thank you."

The ice in her voice told him he wasn't quite back in her good graces yet. He smiled at the girls, then turned to stare out the window. Why was she so upset about his spending a little money on them? If he could just figure out a way, he'd do even more. He wanted to give them all kinds of things, to share with them as they had with him. The problem was getting around Sara's stubbornness. He turned to watch the girls, an idea forming in his mind.

"How about a little game of auto bingo?" he asked them.

"Okay," they agreed quickly.

"But with some new ground rules," he added.

Their smiles faded and suspicion grew, but they followed him to the back of the camper.

"Okay," he said in a low voice. "To make this game a little more interesting, let's make a bet. You girls know what a bet is, don't you? We each have to offer something that we'll give up if we lose."

The twins nodded in unison.

"Fine," Mike responded. "If I lose, I'll buy dinner for everyone tonight in a restaurant."

They looked at each other, silently pondering the possibilities. Finally Megan turned to him. "If *we* lose, we'll promise not to beat you up anymore."

"That's really swell of you two," he said, accepting the offer.

"And we'll also take your turn at washing dishes tonight," Kari added.

Mike nodded and picked up the cards. "Now we're going to make this absolutely fair," he said. "I'm going to mix the cards up and lay them face down. Then we'll pick."

He muffled a chuckle over the looks of concern on their faces. They obviously had not been planning on leaving things up to fate.

He had reviewed the cards and found the one that would easily be the hardest. He kept his eye on it as he put them all face down on the bed and mixed them up.

"Okay, here we go," he said.

"Ladies pick first," Megan pointed out.

"Ladies don't stand on somebody's head and jump on his back," Mike pointed out sweetly.

Two pairs of green eyes glared at him as he picked his card. Still looking daggers at him, each girl picked a card.

"We'll play until it's my turn to drive. Okay?"

The girls nodded and scurried up front to get the best seats. Mike followed more slowly and sat down in the jump seat across from the table.

The time passed quickly, and he was careful to make sure that the girls called out more things than he did. When Sara announced that it was his turn to take the wheel, the girls looked worried. They brought their cards back to the table.

"I found five things," Mike announced.

"I got seven," Megan said.

"I got eight," Kari added.

They stared seriously at each other. "We win," they cried, and started to jump up and down.

"Goodness," Sara laughed as she slowed down to turn into a parking lot. "What's the fantastic prize you girls have won?"

"Mike's gonna take us all out to dinner," Megan shouted.

"Yeah," Kari added. "And we can order anything we want."

"What?" Sara sounded confused. "Someone had better explain this bet to me."

"Mike said if he lost, he'd buy us all dinner in a real nice restaurant."

"That's what I bet," Mike agreed, trying not to gloat at outmaneuvering her again. "They won fair and square."

Sara shook her head as she stopped the camper. "I don't think we—"

"Mom," the girls wailed. "Isn't a bet sorta like a promise?"

"Yes," Sara said reluctantly.

"Don't grown-ups have to keep promises?" Megan asked.

Sara did not reply.

"I think they ought to," Mike said.

The twins stared anxiously at their mother.

"We all made the bet in good faith," Mike said quietly. "If the girls had lost, I'd have expected them to keep their part of the bargain. I think they have a right to expect me to do the same."

"All right," Sara said through tight lips as she got up from her seat.

The girls broke into a cheer.

"We'll have a great time, you'll see. I know just the spot to take you. It's one of my favorite restaurants," Mike said with a smile. "Besides, I do owe you a meal."

"Just remember we have to be at our campground by eight," Sara pointed out.

"No problem." Captain Wonder knew just what he was doing.

Sara was relieved to see that Mike's favorite restaurant was a small, homey place. Neither she nor the girls were dressed for any place too spectacular, and a cozy family-run restaurant seemed just right. She tried to relax and forget her irritation with Mike. Then she saw the prices.

The cheapest dinner on the menu would buy new gym shoes for the girls, and the price of the shrimp cocktail was exactly the same as the price of her wrinkleproof jersey print dress after its third markdown.

The girls did not seem to be sharing her discomfort. Dressed in sundresses that she had made, they were deep in a discussion of the menu with Mike. What would they find to eat here? she wondered. They were strictly hot-dog-and-hamburger kids.

"I'm going to have lobster," Kari announced.

"Lobster?" Sara stared at her. "You'll never eat a whole lobster by yourself."

"Then she can have the rest for lunch tomorrow," Mike said, unconcerned. "You have a refrigerator right outside."

Sara bit back an impatient reply. What was there to get upset about? The girls were having a new experience that they would talk about for years. In fact, their last few days had been filled with new experiences. It had been good for them to have a man around, someone they could roughhouse with as they had with Mike that afternoon. Someone whose attitudes were a little different from hers.

She hadn't realized how much they had been missing, living an all-female existence, until she had seen them with Mike. Her divorce had deprived them of more than just a slightly higher standard of living. Sara decided that she had to be careful not to see everything Mike did for them as a criticism of her and what she wasn't able to give the girls.

"What was that I wanted?" Megan asked.

Mike pointed to an item on the menu. "Veal Cordon Bleu. *Bleu* means blue."

Megan nodded. "But it's not really blue, is it?"

"No," Mike assured her, and turned to Sara. "Have you decided yet?"

"Not quite," she said, biting her lip.

She was torn between sauteed chicken livers with raspberry sauce, the cheapest thing on the menu—which was far from cheap, actually—or snails in a casserole with salsify, which was fifty cents more. The problem was, they both sounded awful, and yet her conscience wouldn't let her order anything more expensive.

The menu was suddenly taken out of her hands.

"How about if I choose for you?" Mike said.

Before she could protest, the waiter was at their table. Mike helped the girls order, then ordered Chateaubriand for the two of them. Sara managed not to cry out in protest. The double tenderloin cost more than a tankful of gas. More than a week's worth of groceries for the three of them. She gulped down some ice water and listened numbly as Mike went on ordering—an array of hors d'oeuvres, salads, and a bottle of wine.

"I hope you have money this time," she said weakly when the waiter had left.

"Afraid you'll have to pay again?" He laughed and reached across the table to squeeze her hand gently. "Don't worry about a thing. Just relax and enjoy yourself."

That was easier to say than to do, though. The food was delicious, Sara had to admit, and the wine went down all too smoothly, but she couldn't really relax. She was conscious of each minute that ticked by, conscious that they were inching closer and closer to the end of their evening and the end of their shared vacation. In another hour or so, Mike would be gone from their lives forever.

The bittersweet moments of casual caresses and stolen kisses would be over, she thought sadly. Never again would she lie awake at night listening to the sound of his breathing. And there'd be no one to tell her with a glance that she looked lovely, or to make her feel like a beauty queen in a ten-year-old bathing suit. She felt like bursting into tears.

It was ridiculous to be so upset, she scolded herself. After the divorce, she had vowed never to let herself become attached to another man. And, of course, she hadn't done anything so idiotic as to fall in love with Mike. No, she hadn't been *that* dumb. She had just become fond of him. They were friends and she would miss him, just as she would miss any friend she no longer saw. In fact, her mental ramblings continued, by the time they got back home, she probably wouldn't even remember much about him.

Sara wanted to laugh. That was such a blatant lie that she didn't even bother to tell herself it was true. How in the world could she have been so foolish? She wouldn't be able to avoid thinking about him. She'd be confronted by his picture as she did her chores—making Megan's lunch, doing the laundry. Every Sunday night he'd be there on the television screen reminding her how silly she had been.

She ate as calmly as she could, not even protesting when Mike let the girls order dessert after they hadn't finished their meals. She just wanted to get the evening over with. She wanted to be settled in their campground so she could start getting used to just the three of them being on their own again. She was relieved when at last they picked up their doggie bags and went out to the camper.

"How do you want to work this?" she asked Mike. "Do you want us to drive you to your place?"

"No, I can get a cab from the campground," he said.

It sounded like something they had tried before, but she didn't have the heart to point that out. She put all the leftovers into the refrigerator and took out the map.

"Now, where are we?" she asked as she spread it

out on the table. The campground just south of Disneyland was circled.

"Banning," he said.

She frowned and looked all over the map. "Where's that?"

He came and looked over her shoulder for a moment, his breath tickling the back of her neck and sending little shivers of desire through her body. Then he reached over and unfolded another section of the map. "Here it is." He pointed to a circle far east of where she had been looking. Far east of where they were supposed to be.

She looked at it, then up at him. "We can't be there," she said slowly.

"Why not?"

"Because I wasn't heading in that direction."

He grinned. "I was driving last, remember?"

She just stared at him, her anger building with each silent second that passed. They were never going to make it to the campground by eight. They were going to lose their site because he had been playing stupid little games again. "You mean you deliberately turned off the route and went in the wrong direction?"

"I told you I wanted to take you to one of my favorite restaurants," he said.

"How was I supposed to know it was halfway back across California? I don't recall your mentioning that fact."

He appeared to be getting slightly irritated himself. "I don't recall your asking where it was, either," he pointed out. "And I don't see what all the fuss is about. If you're worried about the damn gas, I'll pay for it."

He stopped suddenly and glanced toward the girls. Sara didn't have to. She knew they were watching in openmouthed astonishment. They had rarely seen her in an argument. Well, they were about to see her in a spectacular one, she thought. Worry about reaching their campground before their reservation was cancelled, anger over Mike's paying for the gas and buying those outfits for the girls, and plain old unhappiness over the fact that he was leaving them that night—all combined into a wonderful rage.

"I'm not worried about the gas," she snapped. "I'm upset because it's just past seven o'clock."

"So?"

"So we have less than an hour to get to a campground that's at least fifty miles away."

"I still don't see what all the fuss is about. So what if you're a little late?"

Sara took a deep breath and tried to control her voice. Yelling would not accomplish anything, even if it seemed reasonable. "They won't hold our site for us past eight o'clock."

He had the audacity to laugh off her worries. "Is that all? You don't have to worry about that kind of stuff. All hotels have rules like that, but I've checked in lots later and never had a problem."

She stared at him for a moment. "I doubt that anyone is going to toss Captain Wonder out in the street. Unfortunately, we don't have the same kind of pull you do."

"Mommy, where are we gonna sleep?" Megan asked. Her voice sounded close to tears.

Damn! She'd never meant to upset the kids. She flashed a frown at Mike and went over and gave Megan a hug. "Don't worry, honey. We'll find a spot. Don't forget, all we have to do is park. You've got your bed right here already."

"If you're done scaring the kids, maybe we ought to discuss some alternatives," Mike said.

"We haven't got time to discuss anything. Do you know the way to the campground or not?"

Mike flung himself into the driver's seat and pulled the camper back onto the street. They rode in silence for an interminable two hours. She said nothing when Mike took a wrong turn and they had to backtrack. She doubted the extra fifteen minutes would make much difference. And she was right. There was a "FULL" sign up at the entrance to the trailer village. Mike pulled in anyway.

"We're full up, buddy," a man called to him from where he was watching his television.

"We had a reservation," Mike told him. "Name of Delaney."

The man didn't take his eyes off the set. "It's past eight o'clock. We don't hold reservations past eight."

"Yes, but—"

"We're full up."

Mike returned to the road. "Looked like a dump anyway," he muttered. "I know a much better place for you to stay."

"Oh?" Sara said skeptically, wondering if she ought to be worried.

"The perfect place, actually," he said. His smile could be heard in his voice even if it couldn't be seen on his lips. "You can all stay at my house."

Seven

Sara just stared at him. "Your house?" she repeated. "We can't stay at your house."

"Why not?" he asked simply. "I have plenty of room, more than I ever use, so we won't get in each other's way. I've got a pool, tennis courts, and my own projection room. The kids will love it."

They all would, she thought. Suddenly they'd be living a dream existence with a man they all idolized. But if *she* was having a terrible time walking away from Mike, how could she expect eight-year-olds to be able to handle it any better, especially after another few days in his company?

"It just wouldn't be best for us," she tried to explain. "I really appreciate the offer, but I have to say no. We'll find someplace else to stay."

"Where? It's past nine o'clock already. That seems a little late to start driving around looking for a spot."

He was right, but she was determined not to give in. She couldn't, for her sake and for the sake of the girls. It would be so easy to get entangled in his

97

web, to forget about everything but him. Since the time would come when they'd have to leave and go back to their own world, wasn't it better that the time be now? Sara thought. She spotted a campground up ahead of them. "Let's try there."

He pulled in obediently, but didn't need to go any further than the driveway. A "FULL" sign blocked their way.

"Sara, be reasonable," he pleaded.

"There must be others along here," she said, panic rising in her heart. Every instinct told her to grab what time she could with him. Her senses reminded her of the pleasure of Mike's touch and of the further pleasures that might be found with him. There was only one little voice inside reminding her of the dangers, and she heeded it. "We'll keep driving until we find a place with a vacancy."

"Sara, this is stupid," he said, and headed back in the opposite direction. "You aren't going to find anything else tonight. If you want to spend all day tomorrow looking for a campground, you can. But I'm taking you home tonight."

There was something about his words that frightened her. Or maybe it was her reaction to them. "Taking her home" sounded so nice, as if she wasn't so alone anymore. As if she had someone to hold onto during the nights and laugh with during the days. And that was a dangerous dream to linger on. She had to put up a token argument, she decided.

"Just for tonight, then. I'll find another place in the morning."

"Fine."

They rode in silence for a long time. Her worries grew when they exited the freeway and she saw the spacious homes that were bigger and more extravagant with each mile. Mike turned into a street and then pulled into a circular driveway. It was paved with bricks instead of asphalt and looked immaculate. Mike stopped the camper in front of the ivy-covered building—somehow she could not quite call it a home.

"I can put you up in the main house here, or in the guest house around back," he said.

There was a main house *and* a guest house? "Whatever's easier for you," she mumbled.

He gave her a look and got out of the driver's seat. "I'll put you in the guest house. It's a slightly longer trek from here, but you'll have more privacy."

She nodded and went back to throw the few things they would need into a bag. She noticed his clothes still hanging in the closet. "What about your things? Do you want to get them now?"

He laughed. "I thought there'd be time to get them in the morning. Just how early are you planning to run out?"

She blushed, knowing she must sound ungrateful. "I just thought there might be something there you'd need." She stopped, realizing how ridiculous that sounded. "That was silly. I imagine you have about a hundred of everything here."

"You'd be surprised," he said quietly. "There are some things that I don't have at all."

She chose not to reply, afraid of the things she was starting to read into his words. Instead, she woke the girls. Kari got out of bed, almost awake, but Megan was still half-asleep.

"I'll carry her," Mike offered. "You bring Kari along and I'll come back for the bag."

Sara nodded and, taking Kari by the hand, went ahead to open the camper door for him. As they went up the sidewalk, she thought it was almost as if they were a family, coming home late and putting the kids to bed together. The thought was so pleasant, it hurt. Suddenly the door ahead of them opened and a young man stood waiting for them.

"This is Fred," Mike said, introducing him to Sara. "He takes care of the house for me while he's getting his Master's degree from UCLA." He turned to the young man. "We've got ourselves a few guests. Want to get the keys to the guest house?"

Well, so much for the family image. Her childhood fantasies had included a husband and children, but no servants, degreed or otherwise. The cozy little home of her dreams was a far cry from this one anyway. She and Kari walked across the marble floor of the entryway, their footsteps echoing loudly.

"Where are we?" Kari whispered.

Sara understood the feeling. This had to be a cathedral or a museum at least. "This is Mike's house," she whispered back. "We're going to stay here tonight."

"Wow!" was all Kari said, but it seemed to sum it up well.

They walked through the huge living room and out through sliding glass doors onto a patio. The tennis courts were off to their right, along with another smaller building. The guest house? Sara wondered.

"That's the tennis house and my private gym," Mike said, nodding toward it. "There are tennis rackets and balls there if you want to play."

Kari's face lit up. "Can we, Mommy?"

"We aren't staying," Sara reminded her. "This is just for tonight."

They walked through a wrought-iron gate and the swimming pool lay before them. Another building stood on the pool's other side. The swimming house?

Apparently it was the guest house, for Fred went ahead and opened the door. They entered a huge room, with a bar and elaborate stereo system on one wall. Mike walked down the hall, then turned into the first room on the left. It was a bedroom with twin beds. He gently placed Megan on one.

"I think there's everything here that you'll want," he said.

Including a man she was becoming far too fond

of. Did he come with the place? Sara mused. "Looks like it," she said vaguely.

Mike moved across the room and reached to turn on a light. It was an adjoining bathroom. Then he went back through the door to the hallway.

"The other bedroom is across the hall." He led them over and turned on the lights. There was a king-sized bed in the middle and floor-to-ceiling windows along the far wall.

"The bathroom is over here," he said, and turned on the light. The room had a sunken tub.

"It's very nice," Sara said lamely.

Mike nodded as if those inadequate words summed it up. "I'll get your bag for you," he said, and left Kari and her alone.

Sara looked around slowly, still clinging to her daughter's hand. She had never slept in a room this large. Maybe she ought to bring Megan in and have them all sleep together in that huge bed, she thought.

"Mike's house is neat," Kari said, and, slipping her hand from her mother's, she walked toward the door. "I never had my own bathroom before."

Somehow, Sara figured, sharing a bed and a bathroom with the rest of them wouldn't go down too well with Kari. She followed her across the hall and tucked her into the other twin bed, then got Megan covered up. She wasn't quite ready to face her own bedroom yet, though, and wandered into the living room.

It also seemed too big and unlived in for her comfort. She walked beyond it into a kitchen. It was only slightly larger than hers at home, but worlds apart in other ways. There were no school papers all over the refrigerator, and the appliances, all color-coordinated, were gleaming. She peered into the oven. The inside was just as spotless as the outside. But then, did the regular guests who stayed here ever cook anything for themselves?

There was a knock at the outside door and she

hurried to answer it. It would be Mike with their bag. Then there'd be no excuse for her not to go to bed. She pulled open the door. It was their bag all right, but Fred was carrying it, not Mike.

"Mr. Taylor asked me to bring this, ma'am," he said.

Sara barely smiled, feeling as if Mike had already abandoned them. "Thank you." She took the bag and wondered if she was supposed to tip him. She'd never dealt with servants before.

"If I might, ma'am," Fred said. "I don't believe Mr. Taylor showed you the house phone."

She shook her head and stepped aside. Fred came in and pointed out the phone on the bar. "If you should want to reach the main house during the night, you would use this phone," he said. He took a piece of paper out of his pocket. "Here are the extension numbers."

"Thank you," she repeated. He smiled and let himself out.

This was a different world, she told herself. And one she was certain she didn't belong in, no matter how much she longed for its owner. The best thing she could do was get to sleep, then leave first thing in the morning. She picked up her bag and carried it into the bedroom. The thought of that sunken tub was tempting, but she wouldn't give in to the luxury. She'd take a quick shower in the girls' bathroom and then go to bed, she decided.

And, after a short time, that was what she was doing. Captain Wonder clung in sensual familiarity to her chest as she turned down the covers on the bed. This vacation was certainly far from the quiet little trip she had planned all last winter and spring. The Grand Canyon and Disneyland. It had seemed so simple, so safe. No threats to her peace of mind or to her heart. Where had she gone wrong?

"Sara?"

Mike's voice came from the living room, stopping

her just as she was climbing into bed. She paused, wondering what to do. Should she dive quickly under the covers and pretend she was asleep?

But that seemed so cowardly, even if it was what her good sense told her to do. There were some other instincts at work, however, telling her to stop being so foolish, to take advantage of the opportunities that came along, to live a little. She walked carefully across the bedroom and into the living room.

Mike stood just inside the door. He was wearing a robe and his feet were bare. What was he planning? she wondered, feeling her cheeks redden.

"Hi," he said with a smile designed to break hearts. "I was hoping you were still up."

"Just barely," she said.

"Want to go swimming?"

She stared at him for a moment. "It's the middle of the night."

"Oh, come on, Sara." He laughed, coming a few steps closer. "Even in Kansas City eleven o'clock can't be the middle of the night. Besides, I've got my own pool, remember? No one will know."

She would. Her body would. It was already tingling with excitement just at the sight of him standing there. Did she dare go out and swim in the moonlight alone with him?

"My suit is in the camper," she said. Even though her heart was crying out for him, her mind wanted her to hold back, to play it safe and not risk being hurt. Not having her suit was the perfect excuse. Until he held up her suit in his hand.

"I got it for you."

"Oh." She bit her bottom lip for a moment as he walked slowly toward her. Her knees felt weak, her heart was racing, and she was scared. The closer he came, the more her panic grew. She didn't want any man to have such an effect on her. She didn't want to hunger so for his body and his touch. "I don't think I ought to leave the girls alone," she said quickly.

He was in front of her, close enough to touch. His smile was gentle. "We aren't going far," he pointed out softly. "Just outside the door."

"But suppose one of them should wake up, they're in a strange place—"

"So leave the bathroom light on. That's what they'll want to find anyway."

She had already done that, but didn't tell him. She wasn't sure she could speak anymore. She just looked at him, hoping that the hunger in her heart couldn't be seen in her eyes. Why couldn't she control these desires coursing through her?

"Sara," he whispered, "don't you think it's time you stopped hiding behind your kids?"

"I'm not," she protested.

He put his finger over her lips to silence her. "Do you realize this is the first time we've been alone? Really alone? Not just sneaking around while they're asleep or sitting outside the camper while you listen for their slightest sound."

His hand brushed aside some damp curls from her forehead. His touch was enough to shatter all her objections, but she had no voice to tell him so. Her body warmed as her hunger grew.

"You're a terrific mother, but you're also a woman. Let me get to know the woman, just as I've gotten to know the mother."

This time he did not give her a chance to speak, but brought his lips down gently on hers. The touch was magic, making her heart race and her body turn to fire. It had been so long since a man had tried to please her. Tom had never made her feel like this. Now she wanted the pleasure to go on and on.

Her mouth was captured by his and she felt his arms slip around her. He held her gently at first, but as the pressure of his lips increased, so did the strength of his embrace until she was crushed against him. The soft velour of his robe and the thin fabric of her nightshirt seemed only minor barriers to the longings of their bodies.

His hands moved down her back, caressing her and pulling her ever closer as his tongue teased her lips, then slipped into her mouth. She clung to him, her hands doing their own exploring over his muscular back. Her normal reticence disappeared in the face of a passion stronger than she had ever known. Her hunger for him was overpowering. She seemed unable to think or speak, but just to respond to the ecstasy of his touch.

When he pulled away, she felt a mixture of disappointment and relief. She took a deep breath and tried to think straight.

"Ready for a swim?" he asked.

She nodded and picked up her suit from the floor where it had fallen. Maybe the water would cool them both off, she thought. But was that what she really wanted?

"Give me a minute to change," she said, and hurried into the bedroom.

"Need any help?"

She smiled to herself as she changed quickly. She was being incredibly foolish, she knew, but she was going to have a good time. She wasn't going to think of tomorrow or next week. Just of tonight and of herself. She was going to have memories, not regrets, to take home with her. She grabbed a towel from the bathroom and hurried back to Mike.

"That was too quick. I was hoping to have to come after you." He put his arm around her shoulders and drew her outside.

"I have to admit I've never gone swimming at night before," she told him.

"I was going to suggest skinny-dipping, but I wasn't sure you'd go for that suggestion."

The air was warm and the gentle breeze caressed her skin and reminded her of the warmth of his touch. She smiled into the darkness and sat down at the edge of the pool. "Oh, you never know."

"Is that a yes?" he asked. He was right behind her and his hands slid over her shoulders. Possessively, they cupped her breasts and pulled her closer to him, his lips placing gentle, teasing kisses around the base of her neck.

"Actually, it's a 'let's wait and see,' " she murmured, leaning back against him for a moment. His touch brought her a glimpse of heaven, but could not totally erase that whisper of worry from the back of her mind. What was she, cautious Sara Delaney, doing swimming alone with Mike Taylor in the moonlight?

She took advantage of a lessening of his hold to dive into the water. It was warm and enveloped her as sensuously as a lover's embrace. She heard a splash near her and knew that Mike was close by, but rather than look for him, she swam across the pool.

The thought of swimming naked in the darkness with him was dancing about in her mind. It would be heavenly to let the water wash over her and soothe away her worries. They could splash and play, frolicking in the water like children, but that would not be how they would end up.

No matter how they started, she knew they would finish in each other's arms. A few kisses and a moonlight swim were very different from making love, Sara thought. Could she spend the night in Mike's arms and walk away from him without hurting? Could she leave him and not feel any pain? If they had had to meet a famous actor on their vacation, why couldn't it have been Rin Tin Tin or Mr. Ed?

She reached the edge of the pool and held onto the side to catch her breath. Mike swam up behind her. His lips found her neck and he kissed her quickly. His arms reached out to pull her close.

"You'll never get a truly even tan with your suit

on," he whispered between kisses. His hands moved to cover her stomach with their fire.

"There's no sun to worry about," she pointed out breathlessly. The temptation of his touch was more than she could fight, and she leaned back against his body, reveling in the wonder of his embrace. Was that why he was called Captain Wonder?

"Sara." His voice was a plaintive cry, a whispered caress that matched the movement of his hands. They moved up to cup her breasts; his fingers knew just how to turn the warmth in her body to a raging fire.

Waves of longing caused her to tremble. She was through being timid and uncertain, she decided recklessly. She wanted his hands on *her*, not on her bathing suit. She wanted to experience the pleasures that he alone could bring her. She wanted him more than she had ever wanted a man.

Sara turned in his arms to meet his lips, returning the pressure of his mouth as her hands roamed over his back. She held him tightly to her, not making the slightest objection when his hands undid the top of her bathing suit. He tossed it onto the deck behind him, and let his hands savor her softness.

"Don't you think you're overdressed?" she whispered, her mouth against his.

She felt his grin and moved back while he pulled his trunks off. She took the time to remove the bottom of her suit, then pushed off from the side of the pool, floating on her back as the water swirled in sensual delight around her.

Mike caught up with her and slid his arm around her waist, pulling her close to his side. It was bare skin against bare skin, and it felt deliciously wonderful.

"You weren't leaving, were you?" he asked softly.

"Nope, just swimming." She turned slightly in the water so that her hands could reach him. The need to touch him was too strong to ignore. "That was what you invited me out here for, wasn't it?"

He laughed and put both arms around her. Their bodies were pressed together as the water surged around them. She could feel his need and knew it matched her own.

"You can stand here, can't you?" she asked.

"Nope." His lips found hers briefly, then moved to her neck and down onto her chest. "But what a marvelous way to go."

"Kansas City would be shocked."

She luxuriated in the splendor of his touch for as long as she could, then splashed away. The darkness, the delight of his embrace, and the anticipation of the wonders yet to come wove a magic spell around her. She had never felt so marvelously alive, so much a woman. If she lived to be a hundred, she would never forget this night.

Mike was next to her as she reached the shallower water. "Did I tell you I was a swimming expert?" he asked, his arms drawing her against his body.

"Oh?" She copied his whispery teasing voice even though her heart was racing.

"Want to see my breaststroke?" he asked, his hands on her breasts, gentle, but knowing somehow just what touch would ignite her. The tips hardened under his caresses, and waves of fire rushed through her blood.

"How about my sidestroke?" he went on. His hands slid over her sides, thumbs teasing at the edges of her breasts, then brushing down to her thighs. She swayed closer to him, her desires taking control, but he only allowed his lips to linger a moment on hers.

"Then there's my thighstroke," he said.

"Thighstroke?" she repeated with a giggle. "That's one I never heard of."

His hand had reached down and, with tiny

featherlike caresses, teased her inner thighs. "Want me to stop?" he murmured.

She moved closer to him, her body arching in pure physical need. "No, no," she whispered huskily. "I always like to learn new things."

Her body was crying out to him, demanding more and more of his touch. The movement of the water around her seemed a continuation of his caress, the darkness an echo of her reckless hunger. She reached out and touched him, her hands gliding over his wet body, her fingers delighting in the roughness of his hair and the silky smooth magic of his skin.

With a boldness she'd never known she possessed, her hands stopped at the center of his desire. The swift intake of his breath disclosed his pleasure at her touch, and she grew braver. Her fingers danced across his flesh, confident that the fires she stoked were equal in intensity to her own. Suddenly his hands on her spoke of a greater urgency.

"Sara," he said, a desperate plea in his voice.

They were out of the water before she knew it, wrapped in each other's arms. He led her to the deck behind the pool and tossed a long, thick cushion from the chaise onto the ground.

"Here?" she whispered, all her uncertainty and caution returning.

"Sara."

The need in his voice called out to her own desires and, without another coherent thought, she lay down with him. The darkness was a velvet cocoon, embracing them in a sensual caress as his hands moved quickly over her. Her breasts were firm with longing, her body warm and ready for his, but he did not rush in his lovemaking.

His lips moved along hers, teasing the corners of her mouth before his tongue began its explorations. Her body throbbed with answering hunger. His hands devoured her breasts, then moved over her flat stomach, reveling in her softness. Her thighs ached for his touch, demanding his attention. They opened, ready for him, almost shuddering with need when he entered her at last.

Their rhythms joined, they clung together in wonder and delight. Soaring higher than she had ever dreamed possible, Sara knew only that he was more to her than any man had ever been. His body and soul brought her ecstasy that she knew she'd never find with another. The world around her danced and exploded, and only his body within her arms stayed firm and steady.

Afterward, they lay together quietly, slowly floating back to earth. Mike kissed her neck gently. "I've had enough swimming, haven't you?"

Sara laughed lightly. "We've hardly swum at all." She shivered in his arms, more from the intensity of her desire than from the cool air, but he pulled back.

"We'd better hurry inside or you'll catch cold. Too much swimming can be bad for your health."

She let him help her to her feet, finding her knees disgustingly weak. They started back toward the guest house, but she stopped him. "I've got to find my bathing suit."

"We can find it in the morning," he said.

"And let Fred know what we were doing out here? No, thank you."

Fred probably had a pretty good idea anyway, but thankfully Mike did not point that out. She didn't want to think of all the other women Mike had had, not now, not when she was still wobbly from the power of his love. She found her suit and they walked back toward the guest house.

"What if the girls are awake?" she asked suddenly.

"Sara, they were exhausted. Stop worrying."

"But they've never seen me with a man."

He stopped at the door. "Go in and check."

She hurried across the living room and peeked

into the girls' bedroom. They were sound asleep, she was relieved to see. Mike was being so thoughtful. More than she deserved, probably. She couldn't picture any of the men she knew being willing to wait outside while she checked on her daughters.

"They're asleep," she told him.

"Good." He slipped into the room. "It's freezing out there."

Somehow everything seemed different in the house. The lights were on, glowing dimly, but still on. Now she could see his body, and she marveled at how beautiful it was with all the muscles his Captain Wonder suit only hinted at. But he could see her body too. How did she measure up to the other women he had known? Would he make some excuse to leave?

"Do you know how beautiful you are?" he said suddenly, sweeping her up into his arms.

She just laughed. She didn't care if he was lying or just blind. Tonight she felt beautiful, and she needed him to tell her so. She wrapped her arms around his neck as he carried her into the bedroom, and he paused just inside the door so that she could shut it.

Then he laid her gently on the sheets still neatly pulled back from when she had been about to get in, hours and lifetimes ago. This time their exploration of each other was slow and tender, as if they had all the time in the world. This time they watched their desire grow, not just felt it, so that when they came together again, the explosion of feeling was more breathlessly powerful than the first time they made love.

Then, still wrapped in the safety of Mike's arms, Sara fell asleep. She didn't care what the girls would think if they came in. She was too happy, too satisfied, to think beyond the moment.

Eight

"Mommy! Wake up!"

"Is this really Mike's house?"

Sara turned over slowly, reluctant to relinquish the sweet peacefulness of sleep. It didn't seem possible that it was morning already. How late had she and Mike—

Her eyes flew open and she sat up, but Mike was gone. The bed next to her was smooth and unrumpled. It was as if he had never been there. She hadn't dreamed it all, had she?

"Mommy, how come you aren't wearing your nightshirt?"

No, she guessed she hadn't. She got her Captain Wonder nightshirt from the chair where she'd left it and slipped it on, feeling more like her old self. Back down on earth from the glorious heights she and Mike had reached last night. "I was too hot and took it off," she told the girls.

"Can *we* sleep without our pajamas?"

She ignored the question and forced herself back into the role of mother. "Come on," she said, herding them into her bathroom. "How about a bath in that tub before you get dressed?"

The sunken tub successfully distracted them and gave her time to put her mind back in working order. She ran the water while they undressed.

"Can we take a bubble bath?"

"This is Mike's house," she pointed out. "I'm sure he doesn't have any bubble bath." But, sure enough, they found one shelf with a whole array of bath oils and soaps and bubble bath. She poured some into the water, trying not to wonder why it was there or who had used it. The girls squealed with delight at the mounds of suds that appeared.

"Don't forget to wash," Sara cautioned, then went across the hall to their bathroom to shower.

She was relieved that Mike had no longer been in bed when the girls came in, but at the same time she was more than a little hurt that he had left without a word. Hadn't it been as spectacular for him as it had been for her? She had lain in his arms for most of the night, and somehow that was how she had expected to awaken. To *his* touch, not the girls'.

And when she did see him, what was she supposed to say? She didn't have much experience along these lines. Was she supposed to play it cool and pretend it had never happened? Or greet him warmly, as if she wanted the whole world to know?

She was dressed and back in her bedroom before the girls were done. She could hear them laughing and splashing as they played. Probably the best way to handle it was to play it by ear, she decided, follow Mike's lead. And, of course, it wasn't as if they would be here much longer. No, they'd pack up their few things, say good-bye to Mike, and be gone. The thought left tears in her eyes.

She really didn't want to go, she realized. What she really wanted to do was run out the door and throw herself into Mike's arms. She wanted to feel his body next to hers and know that his need for her was as desperate as her need for him. She needed to know that one night together hadn't quenched his thirst for her, but only made it stronger. Her burning for him certainly was still raging out of control.

Somehow she managed to make her bed and lay out clothes for the girls, packing their pajamas into her bag, along with her damp bathing suit. She was just about to get the girls out of the tub when the phone rang.

It would be Mike, she thought as she flew across the room to answer it. He would be calling to wish her a good morning and to tell her that he would have liked to stay later, that he had only left because he'd feared the girls would come in. But it was Fred, asking her to come over to the main house when she was ready for breakfast.

Sara thanked him and told him they'd be over in about ten minutes. Then she hung up the phone and took a deep breath. She didn't care that it wasn't Mike, she told herself. She hadn't expected him to be hanging around just because they had spent the night together. That wasn't the way things were done anymore. She'd see him at breakfast and that would be soon enough.

"Come on, girls, time to get out," she called as she walked briskly into the bedroom. "We're going to have breakfast with Mike and then be on our way."

She ignored their protests and got them dried and dressed and over to the main house in the allotted ten minutes. Fred was waiting for them and showed them to a table set for three out on the patio.

"Where's Mike?" Megan asked the question Sara had been holding back.

"Mr. Taylor had to leave for the studio," Fred said. "Now, what would you like for breakfast?"

"Pancakes," Kari said. Megan nodded her agreement.

Fred left to prepare breakfast and Sara listened vaguely to the girls' chatter. Somehow time had meant little while they were traveling together, but now that Mike was back home, how could she have expected him to be around? It was Monday morning and he had to get back to work.

Still, why would he leave without saying goodbye to them? He knew that they were planning to go this morning. It was hard enough to leave him, but to find out he didn't care enough to say goodbye really hurt.

Fred came out with a glass of orange juice for each of them. "How come Mike left so early?" Megan asked.

Sara stared into her orange juice and listened.

"Shooting starts real early, between five and six A.M. He has to be there."

Megan didn't reply, but Sara felt a little better. Mike must have decided not to wake them out of consideration, not because he didn't care to say good-bye. It was too bad, but it was probably just as well. It would be easier on them all, with no tearful good-bye scenes. The pancakes came and the girls ate heartily while she picked at the food.

When Fred came back to clear the dirty dishes, Sara took the girls by the hand. "We are really sorry not to have the chance to thank Mr. Taylor himself for his hospitality," she told Fred. "But I hope you will convey our gratitude to him."

He looked puzzled. "But you'll see him tonight."

She shook her head. "No, I'm afraid not. We have to be on our way this morning."

"But I understood from Mr. Taylor that you would be staying," Fred insisted. "In fact, he told me to get the Mercedes out for you to drive while you were here."

"I'm sorry if you went to any trouble," she said, "but Mr. Taylor was aware of our plans." Sara was back to being angry. As much as she wanted to be with him, she was tired of his trying to manipulate her. Why did he keep making decisions without consulting her? She turned on her heel and started back toward the guest house with the girls. "We'll just get our things together and be out of your hair."

"But you can't."

Sara knew it was not Fred's fault, but he was getting a bit annoying. Just because Mike had told him they were staying longer didn't mean they weren't free to leave. She stopped and turned around.

"I'm sure that Mr. Taylor will understand," she assured him.

"But you can't leave," Fred repeated. "Mr. Taylor asked me to get his things from the camper and I took the liberty of sending your things to the laundry with his."

"You took our clothes?" He truly looked embarrassed and she found she could not stay angry with him.

"There was a laundry bag with dirty clothes in it," he said with a shrug. "But they'll be returned tomorrow."

She sighed. "I guess we could come back for them." Fred still looked uncomfortable. "Don't tell me, you sent the camper out to be laundered too?"

"No, no," he said quickly. "But it was leaking oil and Mr. Taylor agreed that it should be checked out."

Damn him, she fumed. "I guess we don't have much choice then, do we? We have to stay."

The girls were delighted, and even Sara wasn't as angry as she felt she ought to be. She wanted to see Mike again, perhaps even to know the ecstasy of his arms once more pulling her to him with passionate need.

Mike was back by five, but was disappointed to find that he had beaten Sara and the girls home.

He had been so anxious to see them again. After changing into shorts, he went out and sat by the pool to wait for them. He wasn't there long before they returned looking exhausted. Even the girls' mouse-eared hats seemed to be drooping slightly.

"Mike!" Kari cried, spotting him.

He got to his feet as the girls ran over to greet him. Sara followed more slowly. He couldn't tell if she was glad to see him or not.

"We went on a submarine."

"And in a haunted house."

"And drove cars."

Over the babble of the girls' voices, he smiled at Sara. He wanted to take her in his arms and caress away that weariness. He could bring a smile to those tired eyes if she would just let him, he thought tenderly.

"Can we go swimming, Mommy?"

She frowned at the girls. "I thought you were tired."

"Not anymore," they insisted. "Just hot."

She shrugged. "As long as you don't expect me to join you."

"Great," they cried, and ran off to the guest house to change.

As soon as the girls were out of sight, Sara was in his arms. His mouth came down on hers and he drank hungrily of her sweetness. His hands pulled her closer and closer to him until she protested halfheartedly.

"Mike, the girls might see us."

"And what if they do? Don't men and women kiss in Kansas City?"

"That's not the point."

His hand touched her cheek with gentle fondness. Just having her in his arms wasn't enough. His hands needed to be touching her everywhere, feeling her desire reborn. A current of raw wanting raced through him. Memories of the passion they'd shared last night flooded his mind, leaving an aching need for her in their wake.

He had missed her, he realized, now that she was secure within his embrace. Lost in the wonder of her lips, he could admit that the hours away from her had seemed long and tiring. He had grown used to Sara's presence in these last few days. She had a warm, comforting aura about her, and in one day she had turned his house into a home.

She pushed him away from her gently. "I really ought to be mad at you," she told him. "I'm getting a little tired of having my decisions swept aside by your actions."

"What did I do now?"

"You know I only meant for us to stay one night. I told you I was going to find a campground today."

"So?"

"So that's hard to do when we don't have a camper to drive."

The girls came running out in their bathing suits and jumped into the water. They splashed each other, laughing as they swam about. Mike pulled Sara over to two lounge chairs on the wooden deck so they could talk.

"What's the big deal about staying here?" he asked. "I've got plenty of room, most of it going to waste, not to mention the pool."

She sighed. "I just prefer to pay my own way," she said. "I don't like feeling dependent on anyone."

"I know," he said. "The budget book and no hot lunches or new clothes until Christmas."

She blushed and turned away from him. "How did you know about that?"

He didn't know what there was to be embarrassed about and held her hand gently. "The kids told me."

She still would not look at him. "That doesn't mean we need your charity," she whispered.

"There's nothing wrong with saving for the things you want."

Why was she being so stubborn? he wondered. "Of course not, so why not save the money you would be spending if you weren't staying here? Buy yourself some new clothes with it."

"I don't need any new clothes," she informed him, getting to her feet and pulling her hand from his. "And when I do, I will work it into the budget without your help."

He stood up. "My Lord, will you stop being so damn pigheaded?" he snapped. "What do you think it's costing me to put you up? The only expense is the little bit of food you and the girls eat, and even that isn't much. I could have paid for your whole vacation and barely noticed it."

Damn. That had been the wrong thing to say. He could tell from the shuttered look that came over her face, and he wished he had bitten his tongue instead of speaking. But what else could he say? It was too soon to tell her he wanted them to stay, that he was beginning to feel they were the happiest part of his life.

"Sara, I'm sorry, I didn't mean that the way it sounded," he said softly. His hand gently turned her face to look at him. "It shouldn't matter that I have more money. It doesn't to me, why should it to you?"

"It's not just the money," she said stiffly. How could she make him understand that she wanted to hear him say that he really cared for her? "It's everything. Look at the way you live. What do you think the girls will think of me when we get back home and they see our tiny little town house? How do you think I'll compare to you when there's no built-in swimming pool to jump into on a hot day?"

He just stared at her as he shook his head. "You aren't making any sense. Why should they love you any less because you can't afford a house this size?"

"We aren't talking about 'shoulds.' We're talking about reality. They aren't going to get everything they want in their lives and it isn't too early for them to start learning that fact. There is no Captain Wonder to buy them new dresses just because they want them. Captain Wonders don't exist in real life."

"I do too," he protested with a forced laugh. "Those tights I have to wear are quite real, I'll have you know."

"Oh, Mike, that's not what I meant and you know it. Sometimes I wonder if you know who you are and who your TV role is," she said impatiently, then sighed. "I'm going to change my clothes. Will you keep an eye on the kids while I'm gone?"

"Have no fear," he called after her. "They shall be under the protection of Captain Wonder."

Her stiff back told him that his attempt at humor was not appreciated. The trouble was, he hadn't known what to say to her. He knew that someone must have hurt her terribly to make her so afraid to lean even a little on another person. He wished he had the words to make it all better, to soothe away all the pain she had suffered, but words like that didn't come easily to him. In fact, just the desire to help her was a new feeling. New and a little frightening. He wasn't sure he wanted to share someone else's hurt. Laughter was easier, more comfortable.

He sat down on the edge of the pool, dangling his bare feet in the water. "So, kids, how do you like staying in Captain Wonder's house?"

Sara closed the bedroom door behind her and took a deep breath. She had to stop being so sensitive, she knew. She should just have thanked Mike politely for all he'd done and then said they'd be on their way. There was no reason to start an argument. All it did was make her look ungrateful and ill-mannered. In reality, she was neither of those things. She just wanted him so badly, she was terrified. Her mind told her to get away from him before she got hurt, yet her body commanded her to stay.

She took a quick shower, brushed her short, dark hair back from her face, and changed into a red and white sundress. The girls were drying themselves off when she got back outside.

"Great timing," Mike said. "We were just about to come and get you. Dinner's ready."

"You'd better hurry and change then, girls," she told them.

"We're just eating on the patio," Mike said. "I told them they could keep their suits on."

Sara smiled and said nothing more. This would be their last night here. It didn't matter if the girls ate dinner in their swimsuits. What did matter was that Mike accept her decision this time. They were definitely leaving in the morning.

It was sunny and pleasant on the patio, and dinner was delicious. The main course was steak, accompanied by a cool fruit salad and lots of crisp, fresh vegetables. The wine was a pleasant addition, and Sara relaxed as the kids told Mike about their day at Disneyland.

"Where did you live as a child?" she asked Mike when the girls had run out of things to say. "Was it near here?"

"It was right here, as a matter of fact." He laughed and refilled her wineglass.

"Really?" The girls sounded impressed. "You ate dinner right here with your mommy and daddy?"

"Well, no," he said, shaking his head with a strange smile. "I didn't see that much of them. They both had big careers and had to be where their movies were being filmed."

"Who took care of you, then?" Kari asked.

"Oh, lots of different people. We had servants to take care of the house and nannies to take care of me."

It sounded awful to Sara. She couldn't imagine leaving the raising of her children to someone else.

"Did you have any brothers or sisters?" Megan asked.

"Nope, just me." He grinned at them. "So when they brought home presents, I didn't have to share them."

"Lucky!" Both girls sighed with a glare at the other.

Sara decided to change the subject. "If you girls are done eating, you can carry your plates into the kitchen."

"Fred'll do that," Mike said.

"The girls don't mind," she assured him, ignoring the sour faces on her daughters. They got to their feet reluctantly.

"Who'd you play with if you didn't have any brothers or sisters?" Kari asked as she pushed in her chair.

"Sometimes other kids came over," he said. "Kids whose parents worked with my parents. Or else I'd play with the servants."

"Who probably always let you win," Sara couldn't help remarking.

"Probably," he agreed with a shameless grin.

The girls seemed to be gone only a moment. "Can we play tennis now, Mommy?" they asked.

"Not right after you've eaten."

"Oh, Mom!" they began, but Mike interrupted them.

"I've got a better idea. I just happen to have a copy of every *Captain Wonder* show ever made. What do you say we go inside and watch your favorites?"

"All right!" the girls cried.

Sara was less enthusiastic. "Oh goody."

Mike laughed and led them inside. Sara expected

him to put the show on a video recorder, but instead he took them to a real projection room.

"Boy, your very own movie room," Megan murmured in awe. "It's out of this world."

There were only a dozen seats in the room and the girls settled down in the middle, staring at the huge blank screen in front of them.

"Any requests?" Mike asked. "Or should I play my favorite?"

"Your favorite," they agreed.

"Okay. You sit tight. Your mom and I have to go into the next room to put the film on."

He took Sara by the hand and led her into a tiny room in the back. Once the door closed behind them, she was in his arms again, clinging to him just as tightly as he held her. Their lips met and the fire exploded once more between them. His lips, his hands, his whole body fueled the flames of her passion.

"Still mad at me?" he whispered after a moment.

She had some pride left, even if she was melting disgracefully into his arms. "Yes."

"Mmm, you taste good when you're mad."

His lips came down on hers again, harder this time and more demanding. She responded with equal desire; his kisses made it difficult for her to remember her name, much less her anger. She pulled away from him after a few breathless, heart-stopping minutes, then looked around the film library as if it fascinated her. After a moment she regained her sanity.

"Was this room here when you were a child?" she asked.

"A slightly less modern version," he told her. He took a tape from a shelf and slid it into a machine. After a few seconds she heard the *Captain Wonder* theme coming from the other room, then the sound of the girls cheering. "My mother would bring home movies I wanted to see, along with her current lover. They were a bribe for my silence."

"How awful!" Sara cried, feeling drawn to him, wanting to soothe away the hurt that he must have felt.

He only shrugged and sat on the edge of a table. "My father knew all about them. He had his mistresses. I'd meet them when I visited him on his movie sets. My parents each just thought they were being terribly discreet."

"Why did they stay married?"

"Divorce wasn't as acceptable then as it is now, and I guess they were happy in a fashion."

"Were you?"

He smiled. "Sure, I was spoiled rotten."

She frowned at him. "That's not being happy."

He got to his feet and moved closer to her. "Do I hear sympathy in your voice?"

She was suddenly back where she wanted to be, in his arms. But rather than meet his lips, she leaned her head against his chest. "It sounds like a terrible kind of childhood. This is such a beautiful house. It should be filled with warm, happy memories, not lonely ones."

"I don't think the house has anything to do with it," he pointed out.

She could hear the smile in his voice and did not care if he was laughing at her. So he'd had more money than she had, even as a child; his childhood sounded bleak compared to her own. She had always been surrounded by love. Too much love, she'd even thought at times.

"Besides," he went on, "it's not as if this is a dismal place. Haven't you and the girls liked it here? I mean, truthfully."

Was that why he wanted them to stay? she wondered. To fill the rooms with laughter instead of his lonely memories? "Yes, it's been very comfortable," she admitted slowly.

"Just comfortable?"

She pulled away from him and leaned back against the cabinet. "Physically, it's a marvelous place. I'd have to be crazy not to like it. But on another level, it frightens me."

He frowned at her, obviously not understanding. Yet now that she had her chance to explain things, she wasn't sure what to say.

"You see, I grew up in a very different way," she told him. "We had a tiny house and I shared it with my parents and two brothers. I was the youngest and that was part of it, but I was also the only girl and therefore to be protected from the world. I was my father's little princess, and he doted on me. I was given pretty dresses and a dollhouse while my brothers were being taught how to survive in the world. If someone picked on me at school, they fought my battle for me."

"Sounds like a good life," he said.

She nodded angrily. "Just like what you have here actually," she said. "And it really hurt me in the end. I left my father's protection for Tom's, expecting that he would take care of me the way my father took care of my mother. Only someone forgot to tell him the rules. The girls were born prematurely and were in and out of the hospital for the first year of their lives. Tom was only around for the first four months, but he found them a drag. And he didn't find me much fun either. I think it offended him to have fathered less-than-perfect children."

She was caught up in her own bitter memories and wasn't aware of him until his arms reached out to comfort her. His hands brushed her back, soothing and caressing her as she rested her head against his chest. She felt tears come to her eyes and blinked them back. How wonderful it would be to have someone to lean on, someone who would always be there. It was so hard having to be strong all the time. She felt herself begin to relax.

"Want Captain Wonder to go beat him up?"

The mood vanished. She wanted Mike, not Captain Wonder. The real person, not the comic book hero. "I don't think you have to bother," she said. "He's not worth the trouble."

"Hey, you guys, aren't you gonna watch the show?" Megan asked suddenly.

Sara was already moving from Mike's arms when she saw her daughter in the doorway. Megan didn't seem shocked to have seen her mother in a man's embrace, but Sara felt her cheeks redden anyway.

"You're missing all the good parts," Megan went on.

"Oh, I don't know about that," Mike said, laughing. He put his arm around Sara, and they followed Megan back into the little theater. Kari turned around as they came in, while up on the screen Captain Wonder was locked in fierce combat with a grizzly bear.

They sat down behind the girls. "Say, how would you all like to come to the studio tomorrow and see a real *Captain Wonder* show being made?" he asked.

"Oh, wow, could we?" Kari's eyes shone with excitement.

"Will you beat up the Dark Avenger?" Megan asked.

Mike laughed. "I don't think he's in the scenes we're working on, but there ought to be something exciting happening."

The girls settled back in their seats with cries of "Oh, neat," and "It'll be awesome."

Sara stared at the screen, conscious only of Mike's arm around her shoulders and her earlier decision to leave the next day. Now was the time to say something, she knew, to refuse his offer politely and tell the girls they had other plans. But in her heart she knew she didn't want to.

In spite of all her worries about the differences in their lifestyles, she couldn't bear to leave Mike until she absolutely had to. They had only two more days in Los Angeles. Would it be so terrible to spend them with him?

Later that evening, long after the girls had been tucked into bed, Sara lay sleepily at Mike's side. His arm held her just where she wanted to be, with her head resting on his chest and their legs intertwined. She could hear the beating of his heart, and its steady rhythm was soothing. Her eyelids drooped.

It had been even better than the night before. Each body had seemed to know unerringly how to bring pleasure to the other. Or maybe it was just that after spending the whole evening watching each other over the heads of the girls and touching only briefly, their need was too explosive for slow loving. The moment the bedroom door had closed behind them, they were in each other's arms, clothes removed effortlessly as their passion demanded release.

"Sleepy?" Mike asked. His voice was a soft whisper.

She opened her eyes to discover him watching her. Her hand began to trace lightly through the thick mat of blond hair on his chest. "No," she said with a laugh. "I'm ready to run a marathon."

"Oh, yeah?" His free hand brushed slowly down her back and onto her thigh. He turned her so that she lay on her back, then knelt over her. "I've thought of just the type of marathon you might enjoy."

She laughed, suddenly tired no more. Her hands reached up to pull his head down to hers. She didn't want to waste precious hours in sleep and dreaming. She had only a little more time to spend with Mike and she didn't want to waste a moment of it.

She knew that was all there would be, and she wasn't indulging in silly daydreams of love and forever. That didn't happen in the real world. But when she went back home, when she was alone again and had to be strong all by herself, she would have some wonderful memories to keep her company.

Nine

"Just go on in, ma'am. They're expecting you."

Sara thanked the driver as she helped the girls out of the car. Mike had sent a car to bring them over to the studio Tuesday morning for their promised tour, and she was a little embarrassed by their preferential treatment. But then, so much of this vacation seemed unreal, she was beginning to feel like Alice in Wonderland. She smiled as she led the girls through the double glass doors of the studio's entrance. Maybe it was the remake: Sara in Wonderland.

"Is this where we meet Mike?" Kari asked.

"No, honey. He's too busy to take us around himself. We'll see him later."

The girls sighed in disappointment, and Sara knew just how they felt. She'd rather have him here with them too. They had so little time left together, and it was almost over. It seemed a crime to be away from him for even a moment.

Sara led the girls up a wide staircase, then stopped suddenly as they found themselves in a sumptuous reception area about ten times as big as their living room. A tall, elegant blond who looked like a model in her slinky dress and high heels was at the reception desk. Sara approached slowly, not feeling at her best in her plain cotton sundress and with only a touch of makeup on. She stopped in front of her and took a deep breath, trying to remember all of Mike's compliments.

"Hello, I'm Sara Delaney."

The blond was not impressed. She looked at her coolly through mascara-encrusted eyelashes. "Yes?"

Sara swallowed. Mike had asked them to come; she didn't need to make any apologies. "We're here for a tour."

A frosty smile appeared on the woman's face. "Tours are at ten o'clock and you'll have to go to the south gate."

Sara had dealt successfully with difficult students and irate parents. She was not going to let herself be intimidated by this woman just because she looked gorgeous. "Mr. Taylor said we should come here and I—"

The blond blinked and her icy manner melted before Sara's eyes. "Mr. Taylor?"

"Yes," Sara replied. "Mike Taylor."

"His real name is Captain Wonder," Kari piped up.

"Yeah," Megan added. "He wears a black and red suit and beats up bad guys."

"Oh." The woman was suddenly all smiles. "You're Sara Delaney."

Sara was surprised at the way the woman said it, as if she knew all about her. "Yes," Sara said slowly. "That's what I said." Just what was there for anyone to know about her? she wondered.

"Mike made all the arrangements," the woman told them, oozing affability. "Please sit down. Someone will be with you in a moment."

"Thank you," Sara murmured, and led the girls

over to a group of leather chairs. She was just overreacting, she told herself. Mike had probably said that some friends of his were coming in. That's what they were, after all.

"Hi, I'm Nicki."

Sara looked up to find a short, slender woman standing in front of them. She had long black hair and was wearing a shiny black jumpsuit. Her nails were long, with dark red polish, and she held a cigarette in one hand. Sara got to her feet and introduced herself and the girls.

After drawing heavily on her cigarette, Nicki crushed it in a nearby ashtray. "Well, let's get going." She led them through a door behind the receptionist and down a series of halls.

"Are we going to see Mike, Mommy?" Kari asked after they had turned down the third hallway without another word from their guide.

"I don't know," Sara said quietly, hoping against hope that they were. How wonderful it would be to round that next corner and walk into his arms, she thought.

"Maybe she works with the Dark Avenger," Megan said in a stage whisper. "And she's gonna kidnap us."

"Don't be silly, Megan," Sara scolded lightly.

"They're going to kill us and torture us."

Sara ignored her.

"They're going to drink our blood."

"Megan." Sara tried to muffle a laugh.

"She's wearing black," Kari whispered. "Witches wear black."

"Don't worry. Captain Wonder'll save us," Sara said, then felt her cheeks burn. She was as bad as the kids, mixing up Mike and Captain Wonder.

Nicki had stopped at a door. When they caught up with her, she led them into a small room with people sitting before a bank of TV monitors. "This is a control booth for the taping of a live show."

The girls looked around. "It's *Quiz/Whiz*," Kari exclaimed.

"That's right," Nicki confirmed.

"But we watch this around dinnertime," Megan said with a frown. "And we just had breakfast."

"They're taping the show now," Nicki explained. "This one will probably be shown next Friday."

This time Kari frowned. "Then how come the announcer says *Quiz/Whiz* is live from Hollywood?"

"It's live when they tape it," Nicki pointed out.

The girls exchanged glances, obviously classifying the announcer as a liar, but said nothing more. They all watched silently as the people worked. It was not terribly exciting, Sara decided.

"Any questions?" Nicki asked.

Megan had one. "When are we going to see Captain Wonder?"

Some of the people in the room looked up and smiled. It must be a common question from all the kids that came to the studio, Sara thought.

Nicki just laughed and led them toward the door. "I imagine you see more of him than I do, staying at his house and all."

Sara felt a sudden stillness descend on the room. Every eye in the place turned toward her. She blushed a fiery red, certain that all the world knew about their nights of passion. What must they be thinking? Worse yet, they probably were right. She followed Nicki and the girls into the hallway with relief.

"How'd you know we were staying with Mike?" Kari asked.

"Oh, you can't keep anything quiet around here," Nicki said vaguely, with a short laugh.

"Have *you* ever stayed at Mike's house?" Megan asked her.

"I should be so lucky," she said. Then, in answer to the girls' blank stare, she added, "No."

So that was the way it was around here, Sara

thought, not really surprised. There were a lot of women who'd be delighted to move in with Mike for a spell. Gorgeous, sophisticated women. Then why had he picked her? Did he want a little change of pace from the usual glamor?

She shook herself mentally and took a deep breath? "What's next?" she asked Nicki.

Things went from bad to worse. Every place they went she felt curious stares from the studio people. What had Mike done, taken an ad out in the newspaper, or just had it announced on the evening news?

She could see it now: "Sara Delaney, Kansas City grade school teacher, has succumbed to the fatal charms of Captain Wonder. For the last few days she has behaved scandalously, living in his house and sharing a bed with him. No need to repeat the details, everyone knows them already."

She couldn't decide whether to kill him or just never speak to him again. The trouble was, the moment she saw him, all she wanted to do was throw herself into his arms. Where was her pride? Her self-respect? She simply had none where he was concerned. The overwhelming passion he awoke in her left no place for other, trivial emotions, she thought helplessly as Mike approached them.

"So how was your tour?" he asked her quietly while they walked toward the *Captain Wonder* set. The girls had run up ahead with Nicki.

"Fine," she said after a moment.

"Look, if you had any problems, please tell me. I let it be known that you were special friends of mine and that everyone should take good care of you."

"I wondered who I had to thank for that," Sara said, unable to keep the hurt and anger from her voice.

"What's wrong?"

"Oh, nothing at all, Mr. Taylor," she blurted out. "It's just that everyone in this studio seems to know all about us."

"What's wrong with that?" Mike asked.

Sara clenched her teeth. Why didn't he understand that she hated the stares and whispering behind her back? That they thought she was some groupie who got her kicks by sleeping with someone famous? That she didn't care if he was Captain Wonder or the Wonder Bread man, she'd love him all the—

Oh Lord. She stopped, her mind frozen with horror. What in the world had she done? She was too smart to let herself fall in love. She'd learned her lesson years ago and had vowed never to make such a stupid mistake again. She wasn't in love. She couldn't be. But she was.

"For heaven's sake, Sara," Mike went on, "what are you mad about? You wouldn't have seen much of anything if you had gone on a regular tour. All I wanted to do—"

"Mike"—a short man with frizzy hair and horn-rimmed glasses hurried over to them—"You have thirty minutes to get into costume. Andy's going to take the jump and then they'll be ready for you."

Sara was grateful for the interruption. She needed time to get her mind working again. She was somewhat surprised by the irritation in Mike's voice when he spoke. "Tell Hal we don't need Andy. Hold up shooting until I come out."

"What the hell are you talking about?" the other man asked.

"Just tell Hal to wait," Mike snapped. "I'll see you later," he said to Sara, then hurried down a hallway.

The man sighed and shook his head. "Hal isn't going to like this," he muttered, more to himself than to Sara. He left as Nicki and the girls came back to join Sara.

Nicki took them around the *Captain Wonder* set and showed them some of the special props, then herded them up to a balcony where they could look down on the scene as it was filmed. Sara was rather worried by the exchange she had just heard and was glad when the girls were distracted by the goings-on below.

"Who's Andy?" she asked Nicki casually.

"Mike's stuntman." Nicki went to get some chairs before Sara could ask her anymore. Sara did not feel any better.

"Look, there's Mike," Megan said, pointing.

Sara looked down and saw Mike, in costume, engaged in an argument with a gray-haired, heavyset man. Nicki had returned with the chairs, though, so she went to help her set them up. By the time they were all seated, there was more action below.

"Mike's climbing a ladder, Mommy."

"No," Nicki corrected. "It's the stuntman."

"No, it's not." Sara was surprised to hear the certainty in her voice. Even though they were not very close to him, she was sure it was Mike on the ladder. Something about the way he carried himself, the strength in his movements, the power in his build. She knew positively it was him.

"He can't be doing his own stunt," Nicki said firmly. "Hal would never let him."

"Is he in any danger?" Sara asked, her voice barely more than a worried whisper.

"Mom, he's Captain Wonder," Megan reminded her.

No, he was just Mike Taylor, Sara thought. She understood the girls getting the two mixed up, but surely he shouldn't. He should know his own limitations and not believe the superhero descriptions in his script.

They watched in silence as Mike climbed the ladder to the top of a platform that had been made to look like a three-story building. There was a thick air bag on the ground beneath him. Apparently he was going to jump off the roof. Sara felt her heart stop. Her hands clenched into tight fists. Her nails dug into her palms.

"This is gonna be neat," Megan said.

Sara's face must have registered her concern, so Nicki tried to reassure her. "Mike used to do a lot of his own stunts. It's just that once he got famous, the insurance carrier wouldn't let him."

"Why is he doing it now?" Sara asked.

Nicki shrugged her shoulders as Mike ran toward the edge of the dummy roof. He took a flying leap, turned a somersault in the air, and landed on the air bag on his back. He lay still for a long moment.

"I think he's dead," Megan said, a tremor of fear in her voice.

"Don't be ridiculous," Sara snapped, jumping to her feet.

"Yeah," Kari said, "Captain Wonder can't die. He can't even get hurt."

Sara felt sick to her stomach, but bit back a reply.

"He probably just had the wind knocked out of him," Nicki assured them all.

But Megan was still worried. "What happened to his wonder powers?"

No one answered her as Mike got to his feet slowly. The girls let out a sigh of relief.

"See, he's not hurt," Kari pointed out. "I told you Captain Wonder couldn't get hurt."

Sara couldn't bear it any longer and almost ran down the steps. She didn't care if there was a group of people surrounding Mike or that the set itself was crowded. She pushed through the others until she reached his side.

"Are you all right?" she asked him.

"I'm fine," he snapped. "For goodness' sake, it was one stupid little jump. What's everybody so upset about?"

As he walked over to the director, she noticed a number of the crew glaring at her.

"I hope you got it out of your system, Mike," one of them said to him.

"Yeah. Let Andy do the stunts from now on. You want to show your little dolly any tricks, just make sure that they're in bed." Mike's face turned dark red with fury, but he controlled his anger at the remark.

Mike left the set without another word to Sara. She felt a slight quiver in her lip, but forced herself to still it. It hadn't been her idea for Mike to do his own stunt, she thought angrily. *She* wasn't the one who didn't know where Mike Taylor stopped and Captain Wonder began.

"You okay?"

It was Nicki. The girls stood behind her. Suddenly all Sara wanted to do was go home. To be where things were normal and peaceful and not confusing.

"A limo brought me this morning," she told Nicki. "Is there any chance I can get a cab to take us . . . to our trailer?"

The woman patted her arm. "Come on," she said quietly. "I'll drive you."

Mike got out of the car and waved the driver away before he began limping up to the house. The whole afternoon had been a bust. He had wanted to look good for Sara. He had wanted her to think he was something special, not just a clown who couldn't do anything but pose for pictures. Then he had to go and get the wind knocked out of him in that stupid jump. What kind of hero did that make him?

Fred opened the door for him. "Are you all right, sir?"

"I'm fine," Mike snapped, and tried to speed up his walk. A pain in his side twitched in protest.

Sara must have told Fred about the jump. Probably about how much of a fool he had appeared too. "Where's Mrs. Delaney and the girls?"

"I believe they're out by the pool." Fred hurried ahead to open the patio door for him and Mike glared at him.

"I just pulled a muscle, I'm not an invalid."

"Yes, sir. Would you like me to bring a drink out to the pool for you?"

A nice cold beer sounded great, Mike thought. Just the thing to wipe the disastrous afternoon from his mind. "What about Mrs. Delaney?" he asked. "Is she having anything?"

"A lemonade."

Mike continued out the door. "Bring one out for me too then." Anything cool would be fine. It was really her touch that he needed to soothe his aching muscles and wipe the foolishness from his mind.

He hurried through the gate, anxious to see her and feel her in his arms. She was sitting at the edge of the pool, her feet dangling in the water. The two girls stood by the diving board. Megan was poised for a big jump; Kari was waiting her turn, but she spotted him first.

"Mike!" she cried, and came speeding around the pool to throw herself into his arms.

He hugged her just in time, then caught Megan's hurtling body and gave her a squeeze too. He looked up hopefully, but Sara was still sitting at the edge of the pool.

"I've got one more hug left," he called to her.

The girls giggled, but Sara stayed where she was. He let go of the girls slowly.

"Is she mad at me?" he asked them in a stage whisper.

Kari shook her head. "I don't think so, but she says we have to leave."

The thought was frightening and the smile left his face. She couldn't leave, not yet. He needed her too much. He walked over to where she was and sat down on a nearby chair. He bent down awkwardly to take off his shoes.

"Sore?" she asked quietly.

He shook his head in spite of the ache in his side. "Only a little stiff." She wouldn't want somebody old and decrepit, or unreliable. That was how her ex-husband had sounded. No, he had to be strong for her. He pulled his shoes and socks off and walked over to join her at the edge of the pool. The girls had gone back to the diving board, but seemed rather subdued.

"What's this I hear about you leaving?" he asked as he eased his feet into the water. The bottoms of his jeans went in with them, but he didn't care.

"Vacation's just about over," she said, staring across the water. "It's time we went back to the real world."

"Why?"

She laughed and turned to look at him. "You sound like the kids. They'd stay here forever if they could. Unfortunately, it's less than two weeks until school starts."

"So stay another two weeks," he said. He couldn't let them go, he thought.

"Mike," she protested. "I only rented the camper for three weeks. I have to have it back a week from tomorrow."

"Then you can stay another few days at least," he pointed out. "It won't take you a week to drive back."

"We had some side trips planned."

"So skip them."

"Why?" she asked with a sigh. "It's been fun, but what's the point of one more day?"

He didn't know what to say and just stared at the girls splashing around in the shallow end of the pool. He wanted to get tired of them, but how could he explain that to her? He wanted their presence to become so ordinary and boring that he wouldn't care if they left. That would be better than his constant concern about her opinion of him and his irrational anger when she spoke about the creep she had been married to.

He had known his share of women, and he had grown tired of each one pretty quickly. No matter how exciting one seemed in the beginning, before too long she'd be just the same as all the others. He had to reach that point with Sara. He had to stop looking forward to seeing her again, looking forward to feeling his body next to hers. The only time he really felt alive was in her arms, he thought wildly. If he let her go now, he would be letting his life go too.

"One of my friends is giving a big party the day after tomorrow," he said suddenly. "I'd like to take you."

"I don't belong at a party given by one of your friends," she said sharply. "I didn't belong at that studio. What in the world would I say to your friends?"

"You can talk to me," he pointed out. "And if nothing else, it'll give you something to brag about back home. Carlton gives one memorable party."

"Carlton Bennett?" she asked, sounding impressed.

He wondered cynically for a moment if she, too, was a frustrated actress who would give her eyeteeth—or her children—to meet the internationally known director, but then she dissolved into laughter.

"I'd probably ruin your career for you," she told him. "One look at me in my J. C. Penney summer clearance dresses and they'd throw you out of Hollywood. You'd have to trade in your Wonder cape and start delivering Wonder Bread." She sobered up suddenly and grew silent.

"It's not that big a deal. If you're worried about clothes, I can bring you something from wardrobe at the studio. Dress, shoes, jewelry." He was suddenly seeing the possibilities for giving her all sorts of things she'd never buy for herself. Wonderful, expensive things, not like paying for a tank of gas or giving the girls some cheesy Indian costumes.

"Mike, you can't be serious," she protested quietly.

"I am," he said, reaching down to hold her hand tightly. There was a look of doubt and fear in her eyes that he wanted to wipe away. He wanted to replace it with the one of love and joy he had seen in her eyes each night when she lay in his arms. But now wasn't the time and this wasn't the place, not with the girls just a few feet away. "I really don't want you to leave."

She said nothing for a long time, just stared out over the pool, her hand tightly held in his. "All right," she said finally, sighing. "But it'll only be for a few more days."

"Great," he shouted, and leaned over to brush her lips gently with his. "It'll be terrific, you'll see."

Ten

"You look pretty, Mommy." Kari sighed.

"Not pretty," Megan corrected. "Beautiful. Really beautiful."

Sara smiled at the girls as she took a last look at herself in the mirror. The vivid green dress Mike had borrowed from the studio for her was something she would never have chosen for herself. Certainly the color highlighted her eyes; green always did that. But she had feared she didn't have the figure for the heartshaped, strapless bodice and tier-ruffled skirt which were the height of fashion. Looking at her reflection now, though, all her doubts vanished. She felt absolutely gorgeous, and for once was not afraid of embarrassing Mike.

She had been uneasy with the whole borrowing issue in the beginning. It had seemed fairly straightforward when he had suggested it, but she soon found it wasn't exactly like borrowing a cup of sugar from a neighbor.

The dress hadn't fit quite right, so a seamstress from the studio had come over to make some adjustments. Then there were the boxes of shoes to choose from, all looking brand-new, yet whichever pair she chose would not be returned so unscuffed. Mike had assured her it didn't matter, but it still didn't seem right. She liked to return things in the same condition she got them.

She wasn't too happy with the jewelry he had provided either, although the pearl-studded choker collar and matching earrings were gorgeous. They looked as if they were worth a fortune, even if Mike said they were only costume jewelry.

"They know how to make it look real," he had assured her. "The studios don't want the hassle of worrying over the real stuff, so they buy the best fakes."

She certainly was no expert on jewelry and just put the lovely pieces on, wondering what her fellow teachers would think if they saw her. She took a long look in the mirror. They probably wouldn't recognize her; she barely recognized herself.

There was a knock at the door and the girls flew off to answer it. She picked up the small purse that matched her shoes and followed at a more sedate pace. The girls had let Mike into the living room. He was wearing a dark conservative suit, but his pale silk shirt was open halfway to his waist. He didn't quite look like the Mike she had come to know in the last week.

"My, my," he said, his eyes widening appreciatively as they went over her. "You look good enough to eat."

The girls giggled.

"You look pretty nice yourself," Sara said. He looked different, but that didn't stop her heart from racing or her cheeks from heating up. Her desire for him was greater all the time.

"I like his Captain Wonder suit better," Megan announced.

"I do have to wash it sometimes," Mike reminded her.

After giving the girls a million instructions to behave and not cause Fred any problems, Sara followed Mike out to the Mercedes convertible. The party was only a few blocks away, too close to suit her. There was barely time to be alone with Mike, to touch him and whisper her desires. Suddenly they were there.

A white-coated young man came running over to open the car doors, then drove it off to be parked. Mike put his arm around Sara's shoulder as they walked up to the door and gave her a quick kiss just below her ear.

"I think we should have just stayed home," he said softly, "so I could have had you all to myself."

"It wasn't my idea to come," she replied. "I'd much rather have been alone with you."

A house servant opened the door just as Mike bent to kiss her waiting mouth. They were ushered inside.

The place was a madhouse. Everyone was talking—or was it yelling? Sara thought—at the same time. The rooms seemed to vibrate with the brilliance of the guests' outfits. The wildness of the colors was challenged only by the strangeness of some of the styles.

A man dressed all in black hurried up to them. He kissed her hand suavely, then turned to have a rapid conversation with Mike. She guessed it was their host, but she could hardly hear a word he said. Someone had turned on a stereo, and the music was deafening.

Just as quickly as he had joined them, their host departed. Mike took her arm and led her further into the house. She met a great many people but didn't really try to remember their names. She knew they were not interested in her, and all she was interested in was Mike, so it all worked out fine.

She drank champagne and danced, lost in the heaven of Mike's embrace. She was barely conscious of the noise and people around her. She felt beautiful, and the light in Mike's eyes told her he thought so too. The movement of his hands across her naked back was slow and sensuous, spelling out the message of his desire in ways that only she could understand. She began to look forward to leaving. The magic spell that had enveloped them grew stronger and stronger, and Sara wanted to be alone with Mike to give free rein to the fires smoldering within.

"Love ya, Captain Wonder," the tall, gorgeous redhead murmured as she kissed the air next to Mike's cheek.

"My pleasure, honey," Mike said lightly.

The woman moved off into the crowd on the arm of a short, bald-headed man.

"Is she a fan or an ex-love who just can't forget Captain Wonder?" Sara asked, half-joking. The redhead had been about the tenth woman he'd obliged by having her picture taken with him.

"Neither," Mike said. "That was just business."

"Business? All those beautiful women snuggling up to you is business?"

He looked more tired than amused, although he did try to smile. "This town is filled with gorgeous former beauty queens who come here expecting to make it big. Then they find out they're just one of thousands who have great looks and no special talent. So they scratch and scramble for every advantage they can find. Getting an invite to a party like this is a plus. Getting your picture taken with an established star is even better. Maybe one of those I posed with tonight will be real lucky and get that picture placed in some trade magazine or gossip column. For a few days she'll be a name people recognize, until the same thing happens with some other woman."

His eyes looked old and weary and Sara again

wished they could just go back to his home. Alone with him, she could make those eyes sparkle and burn. She put her arms around his waist and drew herself close.

"Don't you resent being used like that?" she asked.

He just shrugged. "It's part of the game."

Sara said nothing in reply. As much as she had enjoyed Mike's company this evening, she had observed that it wasn't just a party to Mike or any of the others. It was a business meeting and, for Mike's sake, she would stay as long as he wanted. She had just accepted another glass of champagne from Mike when their host rushed up.

"Hey, Mike baby. Horowitz is here. Let's huddle."

"I'm not sure that I'm up to it right now," Mike said hesitantly.

"You're the one who's always bitching about prancing around in those damn tights," Carlton snapped. "This is a once-in-a-lifetime chance. Horowitz is interested in you. Big screen. Straight role. The whole smash. Yes or no?"

Mike glanced at Sara. She read the uncertainty mixed with desire. "Yes, I want it. But I'm not really into late night meetings."

Their host glanced at her. She didn't like the hard smile that creased his face. "What's the matter? Worried about your little dolly?"

"Now look here—" Mike began angrily.

Carlton put his hand on Mike's arm. "Don't worry, man. She's my guest. And my mother always told me to treat a guest like the queen herself." He turned and beckoned to a young man with dark, wavy hair. "Hey, Lance baby. Get your buns over here."

A young man left his companion and hurried over to the host's side.

"Yes, Mr. Bennett?" he asked.

The man turned to Mike. "See, we'll leave her with a playmate. She'll be fine."

"Look, Carlton—"

Sara waved Mike off. As much as she needed him, she knew that she was not the only thing in his life. She was an adult and could wait. It wouldn't be much longer before they left. Then he would be hers alone, so she could share him now. "Go ahead, Mike. Good chances don't come along very often."

"Hey, smart girl you got there, guy," Carlton said. "Listen to the lady." He pulled the still-reluctant Mike away with him. "Give the lady your personal attention, Lance," Carlton called over his shoulder. "Anything her little heart desires. Anything."

Anything? Sara smiled inwardly. What she really wanted was to be lying in that wonderful sunken bathtub back at Mike's . . . with a glass of champagne, some slow, sensuous music, and Mike to wash her back.

"Well?"

Sara stared up into Lance's face and sighed. She recognized him as someone she'd seen on TV. He was probably considered handsome, but he wasn't Mike. There wasn't any warmth in his eyes, or any laughter either.

"So what do you want, lady? You heard the man. You got the key to the kingdom."

Sara couldn't help smiling cynically. "I've already been to Disneyland, thank you."

Lance didn't even blink. "So, is there anything else you want?"

She shook her head. Without Mike at her side, the evening had turned sour. He was the only reason she fit in with these people, the only way she belonged there. She reminded herself that she had sent him off to talk business, but it didn't help. She felt lost amid all these strangers and hungered for his arms even more.

"You want to swim?" Lance asked. "Hot tub? How about a little snort?"

"Snort?"

"Yeah," he said. "You know. A little happy dust. Snow. The real thing, cola free."

"No, thank you," she snapped.

"Maybe you want to go to Tijuana," Lance persisted. "The man said anything you want. I can do anything you ask."

"Anything?" Sara asked impatiently, ready with a suggestion for him.

He nodded. "I know more positions than the *Kama Sutra*."

"I want you to take a walk."

"Where?"

"Out of my sight," Sara said coolly.

They stared at each other for a long moment. Lance's eyes blinked as if he was having difficulty processing her order, but finally he shrugged his shoulders and left.

She watched him go. Being alone was better than having to endure that creep's company. She mused that the funniest thing about the situation was that that very jerk always played the good guy. On television he was the one who got the girl, but up close he was nothing.

Some people got their parts all mixed up with themselves, she thought. They believed the image some director chose for them. She was glad Mike wasn't like that. An uneasy memory nagged at her as she remembered her own doubts about where Captain Wonder stopped and Mike began. But Mike wasn't anything like Lance. He was real, not an illusion. He wasn't just the role assigned to him. The man she loved was flesh and blood, not a comic book hero.

The room was suddenly stifling and she longed for a breath of fresh air. She pushed her way through the crowd, catching snatches of conversation along the way.

"Did you see Geri's nose job?"

"His belly sticks out so much that he has to wear a corset for any full profile shots."

"You call that acting? My dog does better when he catches hell for tinkling on the rug."

"Did you see that blonde Edgar brought? She'd have a hard time doing an impersonation of a bump on a log."

Sara stepped out onto the balcony with relief. It was much quieter there; the only people around were occupied in non-verbal activities. She took a deep breath and looked down at the twinkling lights of the estates below them. The view was serene and peaceful, and she felt herself begin to relax.

She had overreacted. Lance had been such a creep that he had affected her good sense. And she was tired, exhausted really. That didn't help her think too clearly either. She had to have some faith in herself. She had fallen in love with Mike, after all. As silly as it might have been to lose her heart, she would hardly have done it if he had been as shallow as Lance.

The couple to her left broke their clinch; Sara stood still and listened to the sound of footsteps retreating. Suddenly she felt a presence next to her.

"You're Mike's little schoolmarm, aren't you?"

Sara found a precisely made-up woman with long, blond hair standing at her side. "I beg your pardon?"

"I'm Sylvia," the woman said with a laugh that was harsh and grating, rather than happy. "Everyone's heard about you. Mike's school teacher from Iowa."

"I'm from Missouri."

"Whatever," the woman said, gesturing carelessly. "Everything's the same out there."

Sara clenched her teeth but did not reply. The woman appraised her with a slow glance that went from Sara's head to her feet.

"Well, if you make it with Mike, you're going to bring the clean-scrubbed, wholesome look to this town." Again she gave the short, harsh laugh.

"Is there something I can do for you?" Sara asked. She wanted to end the conversation, but she wasn't going to run away. It was pleasant out here on the balcony, and her stubborn streak wouldn't let her be forced back inside.

"Don't give me that innocent country girl routine, dearie," Sylvia said with a sneer. "You've only been in his house a few days and you've already got a de la Renta out of him, not to mention the small fortune around your neck."

"It's from the prop department at the studio. Mike just borrowed it for me."

"Sure, sweetheart. And the Easter bunny wears pantyhose."

Sara's irritation with Sylvia faded, replaced by anger at herself and at Mike. How stupid she had been! Mike had played another one of his little games and she had fallen for it completely.

"Don't get me wrong," Sylvia went on. "This is a tough world and I think you're doing real well for yourself. You've got more than enough around your neck to pay for a first-class flight back to Arkansas."

"I paid my own way out here and I fully intend to pay my own way back. Now if you'll excuse me—" Sara turned to walk around the woman, needing to be alone, but Sylvia put out her hand to stop her.

"Hey, honey. Don't get your dander up." She lit a cigarette. "We all want to tip our hats to you."

Sara refused to show Sylvia that her words were upsetting, and just stared at her in silence.

"I mean, most of us would give a year of our lives just to get into Mike's place," Sylvia said.

"I'm sure he has parties," Sara said dryly.

"I mean like you have. A private party. A real *private* party."

"It's not like that at all," Sara tried to explain.

"Our reservation at the campground was cancelled and Mike just helped us out."

Sylvia stared at her thoughtfully for several moments. Then she took a drag on her cigarette and flicked the ashes into the bushes. "So let him keep helping you for about a year, sweetheart. Then you and your kids will be on Easy Street the rest of your lives."

Sara's jaws clenched in anger. She wasn't sure what Sylvia was implying, but she didn't like the way it sounded. "I'm afraid I don't understand."

Sylvia laughed. "This is California, darling. Why do you think Mike has kept women out of his house? To be a monk? No, he just doesn't want to get involved in a palimony suit. You got a foot in the door, babe. Don't let the bastard off the hook. *Ciao.*" She turned abruptly and left.

Sara walked slowly back inside, feeling limp and deflated. Everything was suddenly all too clear. It was time to leave—both the party and the city.

It wasn't anything Sylvia had said, or Lance, either. It was the whole place. This was a world that she didn't understand or belong in. But it was Mike's world. That was the real problem. That was reality. They'd each had a vacation in the other's territory. It had been fun, but now it was over. It was time she went back where she belonged.

Mike was still nowhere to be seen, but his home was only a few blocks away. She slipped out of the house and stood on the front walk, trying to get her bearings.

"Can I get your car?" the parking valet asked.

She looked at him. "I haven't got one. I came with Mike Taylor, but he's not ready to leave yet. I thought I'd walk back to his house."

"This late at night?" He shook his head. "I know where he lives. Come on, I'll drive you."

Sara was suddenly exhausted, and grateful for the offer. The valet pulled up in a Maserati and opened the door for her.

"Is this yours?" she asked.

He grinned. "I'm parking it for the owner."

Great, Sara thought, it was just what she needed, to be picked up for car theft. "So, are you hoping to be an actor too?" she asked.

"A director," he said. "That's where you need the real talent."

"It seems like everybody out here wants to be something other than what he is," she said quietly.

"Nothing wrong with dreaming."

"No, I guess not." Except that she had forgotten that dreams and reality didn't mix. She was awake now, though. The dream was over and reality was back in place.

Mike was tired and bored. Horowitz was one of the best producers in town and not someone to irritate, but he was not so fascinating that Mike wanted to sit and listen to him for much longer. Certainly not when Sara was out there waiting for him. He sipped at his brandy and let his mind wander.

He hoped she was enjoying herself. That Lance had looked like a creep. Probably played muscle-bound characters without a brain. He thought uncomfortably of his own role as Captain Wonder and mentally changed the subject.

They should never have come tonight, he decided. He should have gotten her all dressed up like that for a private little party, just the two of them. They could have gone somewhere quiet for dinner and maybe a little dancing, but the rest of the time could have been spent where they both wanted to be—in bed. There was a magic between them that just couldn't be denied. And it certainly beat hours of conversation with Horowitz.

What was the matter with him? He had always loved these parties, laughing and playing until all hours. It was the life he loved. How could he suddenly find it so boring and pretentious? Why did he feel he would have to choose between Sara and the life he was used to?

The thought was frightening. He'd always liked his life just the way it was. Sara and the girls were only temporary additions, just some people to distract him for a time, but not people he needed permanently in his life. Or was that the old Mike Taylor speaking? he wondered.

He shifted in his chair and glanced at his watch. Lord, it was almost three. Sara must think she'd been deserted. Career moves suddenly seemed unimportant compared to finding Sara and taking her home. There was a lull in the conversation and he jumped in.

"I don't know about the rest of you, but I'm ready to call it a night. Hope to see you all again soon." He was out of the library before anyone could do more than mumble a good-bye.

He had left her in the living room, but she was nowhere to be seen. There were still couples dancing and people gathered around the food tables, but no Sara. Where could she have gone? She wouldn't have left with Lance, would she?

He went out on the patio but still saw no sign of her. Damn. He should never have left her alone. Finally he wandered out front, only to learn that the parking attendant had driven her home. Double damn.

He drove home and poured himself another brandy. It was too late to go over and see her now, he decided, so he sat on his patio in the darkness, sipping his drink as he ached with wanting her.

Even if he did go see her, what would he say? He wanted to make love to her, to feel the peace he felt only in her arms. He didn't want to talk.

Words were meaningless. Anyone could write the lines and deliver them convincingly. Wasn't that what he was paid to do? But the touch of her lips spoke the truth, and her embrace was the only promise of the future he wanted to believe in.

He was afraid to look beyond today, to know that the peace he had now might not be with him always. The future and promises were things he'd carefully avoided. He had learned that over the years, from his parents, and from his life: Lean on no one, trust no one, and you won't get hurt. But had he ever been really happy until now? He slumped in the chair, exhausted body and soul, until the sun rose and he stumbled in to bed.

Eleven

Sara heard the muted sounds of conversation and forced her eyes open. It was early. Too early, considering the time she had gotten to bed, but it appeared that the girls had gotten more sleep than she had. She wearily sat on the edge of the bed and ran her fingers through her short hair. The hurt of the past night was still with her.

"I'd like to have a bed like Julie Hansen's, all ruffly and pink," one of the girls said.

They must still be dreaming, she thought. It must be nice to be so young and innocent and believe that dreams would come true. Suddenly she felt very old, realizing how much she had aged since yesterday, for hadn't she still been dreaming then? She got up and walked slowly toward the bathroom.

"Do you think we'll get separate rooms?"

"Wouldn't that be out of this world?"

She stopped walking and frowned. How could they have separate rooms? Their town house had only two bedrooms. Where were they going to put *her*?

"Then your snoring wouldn't keep me awake."

"I don't snore."

Instead of heading for the bathroom, Sara walked across the hall and stood in the doorway of the girls' room. They were sitting cross-legged on Kari's bed as they talked.

"Good morning," she said.

They looked up. "Hi, Mommy."

She came into the room and sat on the edge of the bed. "What's the big discussion about?"

They exchanged glances and then shrugged. "Nothing."

"Don't give me that, girls," she said, sighing. "I heard you talking and I'm confused. How are you going to have separate bedrooms unless you make me sleep in the kitchen?"

They giggled and Kari shook her head. "We don't mean now, Mom. We mean after you and Mike get married."

"After we get married?" she repeated vaguely, looking from one girl to the other. Their hopeful little faces stared back at her. Oh, no, what had she done?

She shook her head slowly, guilt robbing her of her breath momentarily. "But we aren't getting married," she told them. "Why did you think we were?"

The girls looked confused. "But we saw you kissing him," Megan said.

"Twice," Kari added.

She sighed. She should have seen this coming. She should have known how Mike's attention to her would affect the girls. Look how it had affected her, she mused. How could she have thought the girls would be immune?

"Girls, lots of people kiss. It doesn't mean they're all going to get married."

Their faces fell, and Megan's bottom lip quivered slightly. "But I thought Mike liked us."

"He does," Sara assured them. "But that still doesn't mean he wants to marry me. You're friends with the people you like. You don't marry someone unless you love them."

"We do love him," they told her. "Don't you?"

"That's not the point," she said, sidestepping their question and ignoring her own pain. "Mike was only offering to be our friend. He never asked to be more."

"Oh."

Neither of them said a word for the longest time. They just stared down at their hands. She could feel their disappointment and moved to sit between them, sharing their hurt.

"I'm really sorry, girls," she said softly. "I had no idea you thought anything like that. I would have warned you long ago if I'd known. We've had some fun and you've got some great stories to tell back home, but that's all."

"Why did he invite us here?"

"Our campground was full and it was too late to find another one." And then she'd agreed to stay longer because she hadn't wanted to leave him, she confessed silently. She had grown addicted to his touch and had convinced herself no harm would come of staying a little longer. Now she admitted her part in causing their pain. "Maybe I should have insisted that we move the next day, but I didn't want to," she told them quietly. "I was having a good time too."

Kari sniffled loudly and Megan crawled across the bed to put her arms around her mother. Sara felt tears start in her eyes and hugged Megan back, then pulled Kari over too. Both girls were crying.

"Don't cry, girls," Sara pleaded. Her own eyes were starting to overflow and she didn't even have a free hand to wipe away the tears. "We had a good time, didn't we?"

"We thought he wanted to be our daddy," Kari said sadly.

"We thought he liked being with us."

"I'm sorry, girls," was all she could say. Her own tears were coming faster and suddenly the girls were comforting her.

"It's okay, Mommy. We don't need a daddy anyway," Megan said.

"Yeah," Kari agreed. "He'd probably just drink beer and burp, like Kathy's daddy."

"Or write nerf checks like our other daddy."

She hugged the girls closer and tried to stop crying, but the tears just kept coming. The braver they tried to be, the more she hurt. Of course they needed a father, and she needed a husband. They were doing okay on their own, but they just weren't complete. Except for this past week, when things had been so wonderful. *Wonder*-ful, thanks to Captain Wonder. Would she ever be able to use that word without thinking of him and hurting?

She forced her tears to slow. "Maybe when we get back home we can have Uncle Joey come over more and do things with you," she suggested.

The girls shook their heads and climbed off the bed.

"It wouldn't be the same," Kari said.

"He wouldn't belong to us," Megan explained.

She nodded and watched as the girls got their clothes out of a drawer. They began to dress slowly, and Sara got to her feet. "I know what you mean," she agreed quietly. "He's nice, but he belongs to your Auntie Jane."

The girls said nothing else, so she went back into her own room. After showering quickly, she dressed. The green dress she had worn the night before hung in the closet, and she picked it up along with the jewelry and shoes. Might as well return them, she decided. The girls were watching television in the living room, and showed no interest in coming with her. It was just as well, she thought. Seeing him again would only add to their hurt. She could say everything that needed to be said, and that was only good-bye.

She heard Mike before she saw him.

"No, dammit. I told you, just coffee."

She put on a bright smile and walked through the gate. He was sitting at the table while Fred poured him a cup of coffee. "Good morning," she said. Her heart lurched painfully at the sight of him.

He glared at her and she smiled more naturally. "Too much to drink or too little sleep?" she asked.

"Neither," he snapped. "I'm getting a cold."

"Oh."

He glared again and returned to sipping his coffee.

"Some coffee, Mrs. Delaney?" Fred asked. She nodded and he poured her a cup. "Shall I fix your breakfast now?"

"No, I'll wait and eat with the girls." Once he had left the patio, she got to the reason she had come.

"I've brought back the clothes you borrowed for me," she said, draping them over the chair next to her. "You must thank whoever provided them."

The frown seemed to be a permanent feature on his face. "There's no big hurry to return them."

"No reason to keep them any longer either."

Sara suspected he had bought them for her, but decided to play along with his game. Confronting him with the truth didn't seem very important anymore.

"They looked better on you than they would on anyone else."

"Thank you."

His frown seemed to fade somewhat. "Maybe we could find another occasion for you to wear them."

"My first day back at school, no doubt."

That brought his frown back in full force. "I wish you'd stop talking about going back. You don't have to leave yet."

She sighed and pushed her cup away. Her stomach was upset from tension as it was, and the coffee wasn't helping. Her hands longed to touch him, to soothe away his headache and his grumpiness, and she wasn't going to let them do either. "Yes, we do," she said. "I'm not going to let you convince me to stay any longer."

He got to his feet impatiently. "You're angry because of the party," he said. "I had no idea that I'd be gone so long. Believe me, I would rather have been with you."

"That's not it at all." She rose from her seat as she tried to make him understand. "The vacation's over. It's time we went home."

"You don't have to."

"But we want to," she insisted.

"I have an idea," he said. "We'll go out to dinner tonight. Just the two of us. We'll go someplace terrific so you can wear the dress again."

"Mike!" She pleaded for him to listen as he moved around the table toward her.

"You looked so beautiful in it last night," he said softly, "I couldn't wait for all my friends to see you, but tonight'll be ours." He put his hand under her chin and gently lifted her face to his.

She went willingly enough into his arms, knowing this would be the last time. His lips came down on hers so softly and tenderly that she thought her heart would break. Her arms reached out to hold him, to feel his body beneath her hands once more, to memorize his taste, his scent, and his touch, so that she would have him with her forever.

She loved him so, and needed him. She could admit that to herself now. Safe in his embrace, she could begin to face the pain that she knew would come. She needed his laughter and his strength, his support and his love. Mostly she needed him to belong to her—and she knew he never would. The girls were right. Belonging made the difference. She pulled slowly away from him.

"I'm already late," he told her. "Or I'd suggest a side trip up to my room. I'll see you tonight." He kissed the tip of her nose quickly, then turned toward the house.

"Good-bye, Captain Wonder," she said lightly.

He turned and grinned at her, unaware she meant what she said.

Twelve

"You girls had better go get dressed, your guests will be here soon," Sara said, chasing the girls from the balloon-festooned living room.

"Okay," Kari agreed reluctantly. "But call us if anyone comes."

Sara nodded wearily. She had been so tired the past month since they had returned from vacation. She just couldn't get Mike out of her mind. He haunted her dreams, making her afraid to sleep. He smiled back at her from T-shirts while she did the laundry. His face watched her making lunches in the mornings and his red and black costumed form decorated notebooks and pencil cases all over her classroom. He was everywhere she looked.

Today that was especially true. It was the middle of September and the girls' ninth birthday. They had chosen *Captain Wonder* decorations. Cups, plates, tablecloth, even the cake was Wonder-ful. The guests had been instructed to come as their favorite characters from the show and the girls had made up a whole series of *Captain Wonder* games.

She was not at all sure she would make it through the day.

Actually, she had been surprised at the girls' choice of a theme for their party. They had been quite bitterly angry at Mike on that endless ride home from Los Angeles, and had stayed that way for the next week. Then, though they never mentioned him to her, their anger seemed to abate. When it was time to plan the party, they'd insisted on a *Captain Wonder* theme and had looked forward to it with growing excitement for the past two weeks.

"Anybody come yet?" Megan asked, bursting back into the room. Kari was right behind her. They were wearing the Indian dresses Mike had bought them. Not quite characters from the show, Sara thought, but close enough.

"Nope," she said. "You still have half an hour before anybody's due. I thought it would take you longer to get dressed."

Kari went to the window and peered out. Megan stood next to her, pushing aside the drapes so she could see.

"A watched pot never boils," Sara said, but got no response. They continued to stare out the window. They had never been this excited about a party before. What was so different this year? She went to stand beside them.

"Why so anxious?" she asked. "Somebody promise you a good present?"

A car slowed down in front of the house. "It's him!" Kari cried. "He's here."

"Who's here?" Sara asked in confusion as the car went by. They had only invited girls.

"Oh, rats," Megan muttered.

Sara took each of them by the hand and led them away from the window. "Who are you expecting?" she asked quietly.

Kari looked uneasily at Megan, who was chewing her lip. "Mike," she said.

"Mike?" Sara looked from one to the other, shaking her head in astonishment. "What in the world would Mike be doing here?"

"It's our birthday," Kari pointed out. "He promised to come."

Megan nodded quickly. "When we were on vacation."

Sara didn't know what to say to them. She sighed and sat down. How did she explain a summer fling to nine-year-olds? "When you're playing with your friends, don't you sometimes make plans for things you're going to do the next day or the next week?"

They nodded.

"Do you always do them?"

"No," Kari said slowly. "Sometimes we change our minds."

"Adults do too," she said gently. "Sometimes adults are having fun and think how nice it would be to keep on having that fun later. But when later comes along, they've changed their minds."

"But he made a promise," Megan said.

"Honey, he wouldn't even know where we live or what time the party was."

"He does though," Kari cried, happily grasping at straws. "We sent him an invitation."

Sara groaned. "Girls, he lives too far away. People don't take an airplane just to come to a birthday party."

"He could afford to, he's got lots of money," Megan told her seriously.

Sara just shook her head. How could she tell them he might not even remember them anymore? That he probably had forgotten all about them as soon as they were gone? But it hurt her unbearably to think that, and there was no way she would pass that hurt along.

"Just don't count on him too much," she said. "Maybe he was away filming, like he was when we met him, and he didn't get the invitation in time."

"He has to come," Megan insisted. "We told everybody he would."

"Oh, girls," she moaned, and got to her feet. "I hope you're good at making excuses."

They went back to the window where they waited patiently until their guests started to arrive.

"Where is he?" each girl asked as she came in.

"He hasn't gotten here yet."

They unwrapped the presents and began the games, but Sara could see Kari and Megan glancing at the clock anxiously every few minutes. The other girls began to look suspicious.

"He's not coming, is he?" one demanded.

"I bet you never really met him," another said.

"We did too," Kari insisted. "Didn't we, Mommy?"

"Yes, we did meet Captain Wonder," Sara said in support. If only the girls had told her of their hopes beforehand, she would have warned them that he wasn't likely to come. She could have stopped them from telling the other girls and adding humiliation to the hurt.

"Then why isn't he here?"

"Yeah, your own father didn't show up for your birthday. Why would Captain Wonder?"

Kari looked about to burst into tears and Megan was ready to start a fistfight. Sara picked up the remains of the game they had been playing and ushered them all into the kitchen. The wonderful party the girls had planned was rapidly becoming a disaster. All she wanted was to see them happy again.

"Maybe his plane got delayed," Sara said quickly. "That happens sometimes, you know. Why don't we have the ice cream and cake?"

"I guess we might as well," Kari agreed halfheartedly.

Sara gave her a quick hug, then got all the girls seated around the table. She sent Megan to get some matches from the living room and arranged the candles on the cake.

"Anybody not like apple juice?" she called over her shoulder, getting ready to pour the drinks.

There was a collective gasp that surprised her. Hardly the normal reaction to apple juice, she thought. She turned around in time to see Kari race from the table into the living room. The rest of the girls followed right behind her.

"Girls?" she asked, puzzled, and went after them.

Mike was standing in the middle of their living room. He was wearing his Captain Wonder costume and looked perfectly ridiculous and perfectly wonderful. Amid hugging the girls and shaking hands with their awed guests, he looked up and met her eyes. Her knees felt as weak as if he'd actually caressed her, and she fought the urge to throw herself into his arms as her daughters had. Nine-year-olds could get away with things like that. A little more decorum was expected of their mothers.

"Hi, Mike," she said calmly, walking forward.

"Hi."

The sound of his voice sent an ache through her heart. She had forgotten just how much she had come to love him.

"His plane did get delayed, just like you said, Mommy," Kari announced triumphantly as she clung to one of his hands. Megan was holding on to the other as if she'd never let go.

"Mommies are sure smart," Mike said.

"They know everything," Megan agreed.

"Sure wish I had one around," he added. His eyes met hers again as all the girls giggled.

Collecting her rapidly vanishing wits, Sara got everybody back to the kitchen table with Mike seated between Kari and Megan. She tried to keep her mind on the party, but found it increasingly difficult. What was he doing here? Had he really just come for the girls' birthday? What would she say to him once all the guests left?

Before too long, Mike had all the girls entranced, just as he had charmed them so easily on their vacation. He told stories, answered questions, and was the perfect guest of honor. He gave gold charm bracelets to each of the girls for her birthday, and Captain Wonder posters to all their guests. And then, suddenly, it was time for everyone to go.

Mothers who came to collect their daughters were equally enthralled by him. Little brothers and sisters were brought in from the cars to meet him until Sara was ready to scream. Was she never to have a moment alone with him?

Finally the door was closed after the last of the guests and she collapsed against it. "I thought they'd stay forever," she said with a sigh.

Mike grinned as he came closer. "So did I."

Then suddenly she was in his arms and he was kissing her deeply. The touch of his lips made her body cry out with delight. Memories of their nights of passion came rushing back as she clung to him. She yearned to know the pleasure of his body again. She wanted to feel his hands on her breasts, her stomach, and her thighs. She wanted to relive the ecstasy of his embrace and the deep peace of sleeping at his side. His hands slid over her back, pulling her ever closer to him, and suddenly she remembered where she was.

"Mike, the girls," she protested, pushing away from him slightly.

He turned to them, not letting her out of his arms. "You don't mind, do you, girls?"

They fell into a fit of giggles, lying on the sofa and covering their mouths with their hands. "Kissee, kissee, kissee," they sang out in unison.

Mike turned back to Sara with a grin. "I think I've got two more kisses to go."

But Sara slid out of his grasp. "Come on, girls. Let's get this place cleaned up."

"Can he stay here, Mommy?" Megan asked, carrying a pile of crumpled-up wrapping paper to the kitchen.

"Here?" Sara had a vision of all the neighbors looking into her windows, intrigued and shocked by the idea that she was entertaining Captain Wonder.

"He let us stay at *his* house," Kari reminded her.

"At his *guest house*," Sara corrected, careful not to look at him. To let her eyes linger too long on him would be inviting danger and temptation. No one knew her in Los Angeles, but here she had her reputation to think of and her job. Grade school teachers were not supposed to have sex symbols for their weekend guests. "And we'll do the same. He can sleep in our guest house. It's called the Holiday Inn and it's about three miles down the road."

"Mom!" the girls wailed.

"No, it's all right," Mike said, making her feel even worse. "I don't want to impose. I was invited for your party and that's what I came for, not to force myself on you."

He started toward the door and Sara panicked. He wasn't leaving, was he? He couldn't just waltz back into her life for her daughters' birthday party, kiss her madly, then leave, she thought wildly. That wasn't fair. Her early suspicion that he liked the girls better than he liked her came back. Maybe he did . . .

"We can't put you up for the night, but you will stay for dinner, won't you?" she asked.

"Sure," he said. "Just let me get a change of clothes from the car, okay? I'd feel a little silly wearing these tights all evening."

The evening passed all too quickly. She made frozen pizzas, a terrible thing to serve a celebrity like him, she thought, but that was all she had in the freezer, and no one complained. They all helped clean up the kitchen, then they played a game the twins had gotten as a gift. Pretty soon it was the girls' bedtime and, although they tried to drag it out as long as possible, they were finally tucked in, the light off, and the door closed. She was alone with Mike at last.

"Well, I guess I'd better be going too," he announced when they got back to the living room.

Now? So early? "Oh?" was all she could manage.

"It's been a long day," he explained. "And a rough couple of weeks. You look pretty pooped yourself. Probably wouldn't hurt you to get to bed early."

That was what she had hoped to do, but not to go to sleep. Unfortunately, though her mouth opened and shut a few times, she was completely speechless.

Mike came over and gave her a quick peck on the cheek. "That's for the party and the dinner. I'll be seeing you."

"Mike!" she cried finally.

But he just smiled and let himself out.

Sara had thought the previous nights of missing Mike were bad, but the night after the party was far worse. Thinking of him, knowing he was in the same town—had been in the same house even, but had left—was unbearable. Her body longed for him, needed him so badly that she wanted to cry. If she had known what hotel he was staying at, she might have called him. Instead, she pretended to sleep, fixed breakfast for the girls, and got them all off to school.

Even though Kari and Megan did not attend the school where she taught, word had gotten around.

"Is it true?" her students asked her. "Did Captain Wonder really come to your house?"

It was almost impossible to get them to concentrate on their math, almost as impossible as it was for her to concentrate. Finally, she made up Captain Wonder problems for them to solve. In spelling, she had them write a story about Captain

Wonder, using their spelling words for the week. Was she never to escape from the man?

Around eleven o'clock, in the middle of the reading lesson, there was a knock at the door, and in walked Captain Wonder. She had been expecting it, fearing it, wanting it all morning. Her class reacted predictably, moving from shocked silence to an uproar in the space of about two seconds.

"Boys and girls," she cried, trying to get them under control. She had a sudden urge to strangle Mike, but since he was carrying a huge bouquet of roses, she doubted that she would. "Boys and girls, if you can't be quiet, I'll have to ask Captain Wonder to leave."

"I will too," Mike said. The silence that descended as soon as he spoke made his voice seem loud. "I certainly wouldn't want to interfere with your assignments."

"That's okay," one wisecracking student said.

Mike didn't join the other students in laughing at the joke and pretty soon the giggles faded away. "I was told this was the best third grade class in Kansas City," he said. "Maybe I got the wrong room. It could be the third grade class next door."

"No, this is it," they all cried, not willing to give him up to the other third graders. Suddenly they were all sitting up taller and paying close attention. Mike watched them silently for a moment, then turned to Sara and handed her the flowers.

"I hope these make up for the inconvenience of having me drop by," he said.

"Certainly," she murmured. She was barely able to hold the bouquet. There had to be three dozen long-stemmed red roses. "Kathy, want to see if there are some vases in my locker?"

While she waited for her student to find something to put the flowers in, she cast a cautious glance at Mike. He was smiling at the students, but suddenly he turned and caught her gaze. He winked, causing her to blush. Lord, what was he doing here? she thought.

Kathy came back with two coffee cans. Not exactly lead crystal, but they'd have to do. Sara sent another student with Kathy to get some water, and carefully laid the flowers on her desk. She cleared her throat, hoping that she wouldn't sound like a fool.

"And to what do we owe the honor of this visit?" she asked. Why did he have to look so incredibly gorgeous in that dopey costume? A grown man should look ridiculous in tights and a cape.

"I'm on a quest," he said. His eyes caressed her for a moment, then he turned back to the class. "I've heard that the Dark Avenger has caught some of my loyal fans and is making them misbehave."

Several of the students turned around and stared at poor Billy Bailey, who was constantly getting into trouble. "Surely you don't suspect anyone in here," Sara said.

"I'm not sure. If it's all right with you, I'll just sit in the back of the room and keep my eyes open."

It wasn't all right with her, but what could she say with all her students watching him adoringly? She feared that the same look was in her eyes, and briskly told him he was more than welcome to watch out for the Dark Avenger's spies. She asked Billy to carry her chair to the back of the room for him, and went on with her teaching.

Or tried to go on. It was far from easy, feeling his eyes on her, wanting to look at him, but knowing she shouldn't. The next forty-five minutes seemed the longest of her life and she was immensely relieved when the lunch bell rang.

"I think you've got a good bunch of students here, Mrs. Delaney," Mike announced solemnly, and produced a small bag of Captain Wonder Warrior pins. "Maybe if they'll all wear these, we'll chase the Dark Avenger away for good."

The students promised to wear the pins and

work hard. Mike took one out of the bag. "I think we should start with Mrs. Delaney, don't you?"

Of course they all agreed. They'd agree to anything that would make her blush so.

Mike walked over with the pin and carefully put it on her. In order to protect her skin, one hand slid inside her collar as he stuck the point through the fabric. His hand lingered just a moment in the gentlest of caresses. Her blush deepened and a giggle was heard from the back of the room.

"Mrs. Delaney will give yours out after lunch," he said, stepping back from her. "Then you'll all be Captain Wonder Warriors and always have to work your hardest."

He waved to all of them, winked at her, and was gone. If it weren't for the roses, the bag of Captain Wonder pins, and her racing heart, she'd think it had all been a dream. What was he doing?

The next day Captain Wonder appeared next to Sara in the grocery store. He carried on a pleasant, chatty conversation with her as she went up and down the aisles, paying only slight attention to the squeals of delight from the youngsters in the store.

Wednesday, he drove the girls to their Girl Scout meeting and Thursday he pulled into the gas station right after her. She was beginning to feel haunted by a red and black monster, and was getting a little annoyed.

It had been wonderful to see him on Sunday, and amusing on Monday. But it was no longer so. Her body was tense with desire and her nerves were on edge. She had had it with Captain Wonder. She didn't know what kind of game he was playing, but whatever it was, it wasn't funny.

"Just what are you doing?" she hissed at him as she took the nozzle from the gas pump.

"Filling my tank," he said mildly, and took the nozzle from the pump next to hers.

"Why here? Why now?"

"Why not?"

She glared at him, feeling close to tears. Why was he doing this to her? Was this all some sort of joke? She shoved the nozzle into her gas tank and watched the numbers fly by on the pump.

"Sara."

She refused to look at him.

"Sara. Have dinner with me."

"Why?"

"Come on, Sara," he pleaded, touching her arm gently.

She had not expected the brief caress, and a shiver of need went through her. She kept her eyes on the pump. "Don't you feel silly parading all over town in that outfit?"

"Don't you feel silly talking to a gas pump?"

She tried not to smile but it didn't work. Her eyes went to his of their own accord. "What are you doing, Mike?" she asked. "What do you want?"

"What do I want? That's simple," he said. His voice was quiet but his eyes were dark with desire. "I want you to come back to Los Angeles with me."

For a long moment she could not believe that she'd heard him right. "Come back?" she repeated. "What for?"

He smiled and took a step closer. "Come on, Sara. We both know what for. You can't hide anything from Captain Wonder."

It was just too much. She had fallen hopelessly in love with a guy who wore tights and thought he was a superhero. "You may not have noticed, but I have two children I'm responsible for." There was a screech of tires from the street as someone spotted Mike. "Plus a job and a house. My whole life is here," she said quickly, before the passing fans could interrupt.

"I never meant for you to leave the kids here," he said. "Of course they'll come with you, but you can sell the house and quit your job. I've got more than enough money for all of us."

A car pulled into the gas station behind her. She didn't need to turn around to know there were Captain Wonder fans in it. Their screams of excitement were evidence enough. Thankfully, the pump had reached the ten-dollar mark and she shut it off.

"I see," she snapped. "Captain Wonder's kept woman. That'd make a great new character for the show, wouldn't it?"

"Sara!" he protested.

"Say, buddy, are you really Captain Wonder?" The attendant came running out of the station as the kids came pouring out of the car. The place seemed to be swarming with Captain Wonder Warriors and she was quite willing to leave to make room for more. She shoved the ten-dollar bill into the attendant's hand.

"Sara, wait!" Mike cried, but she was going home. She had a million things to do—make dinner, do the laundry, have a good cry.

"Are you okay, Mommy?" Megan asked quietly.

"I'm fine," Sara said, and brushed the tears away with the back of her hand. She grabbed an onion from the basket and began peeling it. "It's the onions. They always make me cry."

Neither girl mentioned the fact that she had been crying since she'd returned to the house, long before she'd started peeling any onions, but Sara knew they were thinking it.

"Want to get me a can of tomatoes and a can of tomato paste?" she asked, forcing brightness into her voice. "I have a taste for spaghetti tonight."

The excitement that usually followed such an announcement was missing. The girls got the cans for her, but their eyes were worried.

"Did you see Mike today?" Kari asked.

"You mean Captain Wonder? Yes, I did." Sara dumped the chopped onions into the pot and stirred them briefly. There was no Mike, she thought. Just a character some scriptwriter had created. By the time she looked back at the girls, though, she had put a smile on her face. "He was at the gas station the same time I was. Wasn't that a coincidence?"

"Is he going back home soon?"

Sara began to brown the meat carefully, keeping her eyes on the pot so she could blink back the tears as they came. "I imagine. He can't stay here forever," she pointed out briskly.

"I wish he could."

So did she, but she forced back the thought and concentrated on her spaghetti sauce. Maybe she'd make some brownies for dessert too. Calories were good for fighting depression. By the time the sauce was simmering slowly, the girls had gone off to the living room, and she started on her brownies.

She knew the girls were upset. They were as fond of Mike as she was. She stopped and frowned. Hell, why not be honest? They all loved him. He was something they all needed in their lives. But not on his terms. If she had only herself to think about, she might consider his suggestion, but she wasn't alone. She had the girls and that was no sort of life for them. They needed security, needed to be loved by someone who wouldn't abandon them.

She was measuring cocoa when the doorbell rang. She froze, listening as the girls went to answer it.

"Hi, Mike." The door closed.

"Your mom here?"

"Yep." She could hear the uncertainty in their voices.

"She still mad at me?"

She had never been mad at him, that was the problem. She loved him too much. She had been hurt, that was all, and she didn't want to be hurt anymore.

"I know you girls told me she didn't like Captain Wonder, but I forgot. I thought maybe she had changed her mind."

"I don't think so," Megan said slowly. "She hasn't watched Captain Wonder since we got back."

Kari agreed. "She likes you a lot, but she thinks your show is dumb."

Sara closed her eyes. When did discretion become a natural tendency? she wondered. She grabbed the bag of nuts and began to chop as the sound of footsteps came closer to the kitchen.

"Hi." Mike's voice was quiet, uncertain, and he was no longer in his costume.

"Hi." Her voice sounded harsh from the effort not to cry. Two tears slipped out, though, and she kept her head down. Maybe he wouldn't notice them.

"The onions are making her cry," Megan pointed out helpfully.

"Oh."

She kept on chopping, hoping he wouldn't notice they were nuts, not onions. After a moment she gained a small measure of courage. "Girls, why don't you go outside and play?"

"That's okay, Mom. We'll stay here and help you."

Help her how? Throw Mike out if he made her cry again? Her heart warmed and she was able to smile at them.

"That's all right, girls. Dinner won't be ready for another hour, and Mike and I have some things we need to talk about by ourselves."

They hesitated. Then they threw Mike a warning glance and came over and gave her a hug and a kiss before they left the room. Sara's eyes misted over.

"I guess I've been warned," Mike noted.

"They're just worried. Mothers aren't supposed to get upset."

"I thought it was the onions."

"Right," she said with a weak laugh. "I always put onions in brownies."

Neither of them spoke for a long moment. She went on with her mixing, while he watched.

"Any chance that the girls are right?" he asked quietly.

"About what?"

"That it's Captain Wonder you're mad at, not me."

She gave him a look and went over to the refrigerator for some eggs. "I'm beginning to wonder if there's a difference."

His smile was tentative. "Sure there is. He's the jerk that specializes in saying the wrong things. He's just so used to having his lines written out for him I guess he can't think for himself."

"Right." She broke the eggs into the bowl and threw the shells into the garbage. The room seemed very quiet.

"I guess I really blew things, didn't I?" he said after a moment.

She didn't know how to answer that, other than with a resounding yes, so she just began to stir the batter briskly.

"Would it help to say I'm sorry?"

"It doesn't matter," she said quietly, knowing that it was a lie. It had hurt. A lot. She stooped down to get a baking pan, but also to hide the sudden tears that had come to her eyes. When she stood up again, Mike was right behind her.

"I just had this crazy idea," he went on, his hands sliding gently over her bare arms, his breath soft and warm against her hair. "I thought I would come here and do things right. When we were in that damn camper, everything was wrong. I couldn't say or do the things I wanted to. Partly because the kids were there, but then, too, because I was your guest. I was supposed to behave."

She smiled slightly, but said nothing.

"When we got to my place, everything seemed to explode. There wasn't any time for taking you out or trying to show you how I felt." His arms slid around her, pulling her closer to him. "We just. . ."

"Made love," she finished for him.

"Yes." He was silent again for a time. "Then, when I got the invitation to the girls' party, it seemed like I was getting a second chance. I had this stupid idea that I would come here and court you—bring you flowers, take you to dinner, the whole bit, instead of just jumping into bed. I thought things were going pretty well until this afternoon. What did I do wrong?"

She turned in his arms, resting her head against his chest. "Oh, Mike," she said, sighing. "We're just too different. The worlds we live in are too far apart."

"They don't have to be." His hand touched her hair gently, in a caress of such tenderness that it almost hurt. But it didn't change things.

"Sure, I could quit my job, sell the house, and move in with you." Her voice was bitter. "Except that wouldn't solve our problems."

"No, but I'm not asking you to make all the sacrifices. I've already talked to a realtor about selling my house."

She pulled back from him and stared up into his face. "The home where you grew up? Why?"

"It's not exactly filled with happy memories," he said. "And I'm not sure that it's the best place for kids to grow up."

She was so astonished, she didn't know what to say.

"I looked at a couple of places outside the city. Ten-to-twenty-acre spreads where the kids could even have some horses, but it would still be pretty close to the studio."

Horses? Lord, she was lucky the girls weren't around to hear all this. "Mike, I really do appreciate all that you're willing to do," she said slowly, stepping back so that she was out of his arms. "But it still wouldn't work. I'm old-fashioned, I guess, but I need more than a ten-acre piece of property, and so do the girls. We need security and commitment more than horses."

He looked confused. "Hell, what do you think I'm offering? I'll admit that marriage scares me after seeing the way my parents lived, but I need a commitment too. Damn, you don't know what it was like to come home from the studio that day and find you gone. I never want to go through that again."

He looked so hurt that she went into his arms without thinking. She wrapped her arms around him and held him close. "I had to go," she whispered. "The girls had grown too dependent on you, and so had I. I needed to keep them from getting too hurt."

"I didn't even know your address," he said. "All I knew was that you lived in Kansas City, and since I couldn't find you listed in the phone book, I told my publicity manager that I wanted to schedule a whole bunch of personal appearances here. I figured you and the girls would have to show up at one of them. Then I got the party invitation from Kari and Megan. I'm forever in their debt."

"I think they'll settle for horses," she said dryly.

He stood very still, then looked at her with loving eyes. "Does that mean you'll marry me?" he asked.

"Of course I will," she said with a smile. "I love you so much, it hurts, but—"

She was interrupted by a long and thorough kiss that made her heart race and her knees weaken. She clung to him for support even as she pulled her mouth away. It was a moment before she had breath to speak.

"It would have been a lot simpler if you had just come here like a regular person and asked me to marry you," she said. "I thought you just wanted me to move in for a while, and I couldn't do that with the girls."

He grinned sheepishly. "I told you I'm better when someone writes my lines for me. And I only came as Captain Wonder to impress the girls. I thought that if they were on my side, maybe you'd come around faster."

"That's sneaky."

He turned serious. "I never realized I could love or need someone as much as I do you. I was even considering taking out ads telling all of Kansas City that you had stayed with me in Los Angeles, hoping to create a scandal that would force you to marry me."

"And I thought Captain Wonder was supposed to be honorable."

"He will be from now on," Mike promised. "He'll do anything if you'll stop being mad at him."

"I was never all that mad," she admitted. "In fact, my Captain Wonder nightshirt is getting worn out from all the use it's been getting."

"Are you wearing it inside out?"

Her blush was apparently enough of an answer for him. He laughed loudly and pulled her back into his embrace. His lips met hers, and she could barely believe that her dreams were all coming true.

There was a small explosion of giggles behind them. "Does this mean you aren't mad at Mike anymore?"

They pulled apart, and Sara smiled at the girls. "Yes."

"Then can he stay for dinner?"

She nodded, smiling at Mike. "In fact, I think you'd better get used to setting four places at the table from now on."

There was a whoop of pure joy and then the girls flew at them, hugging them both.

Sara's eyes met Mike's over the top of the girls'

heads. "Looks like we all love you, Captain Wonder."

EDITOR'S CORNER

LOVE LIFTS US UP WHERE WE BELONG!

You'll be seeing these words a lot in the next six months in advertisements in major women's magazines and other publications. We've adopted this slogan for our second anniversary which we celebrate with the publication of next month's LOVESWEPTS. And we think it's just right! LOVE LIFTS US UP WHERE WE BELONG expresses the reactions of readers to LOVESWEPT romances while describing the performance of our books on chain and independent bookstore bestseller lists.

Now, as we enter our third year of publication, I want to thank everyone who has helped create this remarkable line: you who buy the books, our wonderful authors, and, of course, my colleagues at Bantam, all of whom are first-rate. Especially, though, I must single out the contributions of the LOVESWEPT staff— Susann Koenig, Elizabeth Barrett and Barbara Alpert. Their enthusiasm, excitement, and energy are as high today as when we worked on the first manuscript we purchased for LOVESWEPT. Happy birthday to us all!

Now to the treats in store for you next month.

Sara Orwig is back with a simply wonderful love story, **CALHOUN AND KID,** LOVESWEPT #91. An ornery hero (who is also a hunk, by the way), Jared Calhoun plagues Courtney Meade. Single parents with sons the same age, Jared and Courtney would seem to have everything in common, yet their personalities appear to be completely at odds. She's shy and sweet; he's forward and crusty. It's double trouble from the moment they meet and Courtney gets the blame for Jared being shot in the foot! Then it's more merry and sensuous excitement as they reconcile their feuding boys and set about reforming one another . . . in the most delightful ways! This is another heartwarming story from our own Sara Orwig who just keeps topping herself with every book she writes!

We are delighted to welcome Carole Nelson Douglas as a LOVESWEPT author. A marvelously versatile writer, Carole is known for her historical and science fiction novels. How glad we are to have tempted her to do her first short contemporary romance for us because **AZURE DAYS, QUICKSILVER NIGHTS,** LOVESWEPT #92, is a fabulous love story. Set in Monte Carlo and on the Riviera amidst the rich, the famous, the dangerous, **AZURE DAYS, QUICKSILVER NIGHTS** is the dramatic story of Chrystal Remy, heiress to a crumbling villa and a mountain of debts, and the magnetic Damon Vance, a man known in international art circles for his expertise . . . and mystery. Both have known tragic first marriages, both know what they could mean to one another, but intriguing secrets keep them apart—while forcing them together. **AZURE DAYS, QUICKSILVER NIGHTS** is a memorable contribution to the LOVESWEPT series and a love story you won't soon forget. (Incidentally, some of the exquisite antique clothes described in the book come from Carole's own wardrobe . . . and how I covet those gorgeous creations!)

I guarantee you'll be absolutely charmed by **PRACTICE MAKES PERFECT,** LOVESWEPT #93, by Kathleen Downes. This is Kathleen's second LOVESWEPT and it is a double delight. Pippi and Jeremy are best friends. Unlucky in love, Pippi has always relied on Jeremy . . . and his strong shoulder to cry on. Out of the blue he asks her to help him figure out how to court the woman he loves . . . and Pippi's emotional world turns upside down. She never knew she could be so distressed . . . or enthralled. As their "rehearsals" become more intimate, Pippi finds herself in a dilemma. You'll relish the deviousness of a darling man and the woman he would make his darling, so be sure to read **PRACTICES MAKES PERFECT**! It's fun, it's frolicksome, it's wonderfully touching.

There's humor galore plus sensuous magic in **WAITING FOR PRINCE CHARMING**, LOVESWEPT #94, by Joan Elliott Pickart. You'll revel in the romance of Chelsey Star and Mitch Brannon, two of the most lovable characters in Joan's extensive repertoire. Chelsey is hardly the traditional Cinderella waiting for a fairy godmother; she's an active, vital modern woman. But it *is* glass that brings her together with her Prince Charming—not the glass of a slipper, but of a broken windshield on Mitch's fabulously expensive, brand-new sports car. And there aren't any evil stepsisters here—just a group of wonderful humans and animals who delightfully propel and complicate Mitch and Chelsey's loving fairytale. Another real winner from Joan Elliott Pickart!

Again, thank you for your wonderful support for the last two years. You can count on us to do our very best always to give you the very best in romance novels!

Sincerely,

Carolyn Nichols

Carolyn Nichols
Editor
LOVESWEPT
Bantam Books, Inc.
666 Fifth Avenue
New York, NY 10103

Read this special preview of

THE FOREVER DREAM

---

by Iris Johansen

Coming in May 1985 from Bantam Books

*HE PROMISES NOTHING LESS THAN LOVE
WITHOUT END . . .*

*Exquisite, radiant Tania Orlinov—incom-
parable prima ballerina, renowned Soviet
defector—she expresses the dreams of love
only dance can reveal . . . but seeks none
of them for herself.*

*Brilliant, mysterious Jared Ryker—an un-
common man with extraordinary vision, a
gifted genetic scientist—he holds the key to
an astonishing secret . . . and yearns to
share it with one special woman.*

*She has become his obsession. He longs to
possess her with an enduring passion that
time can never destroy. But when she is
brought to him against her will by those who
covet his secret, Jared is torn by need . . .
and seduced by her beauty. Inevitably, desire flames between them—stunning them
both with its depth and intensity. But their
private fantasy is shattered—by men determined to seize Jared's research and control
its power. Until, in a fierce confrontation set
against a windswept mountain's splendor,
Jared and Tania must fight for their lives
. . . and for their freedom to build a future
in each other's arms. . . .*

Iris Johansen's
THE FOREVER
DREAM

*D*amn this moonlight! Was it only last night she had blamed the full moon for her temporary madness? She was going to blame it for considerably more than that if those clouds didn't oblige. She needed the cover of darkness to cross the courtyard and get around the curve in the road before the guard completed his rounds.

She shrank against the stone wall, deep in shadow. Her gaze was fixed worriedly on the sky, watching the clouds; they approached the moon with a laziness that stretched her nerves to the limit. The guard should be back around to the courtyard in another four minutes, according to her calculations. She'd spent three hours here in the shadows four nights ago, observing and timing the guard's movements. If she hadn't had an opportunity to sneak into the back of the van, she'd wanted to be prepared to go out on foot, as she was doing now . . . as she *would* be doing now if those clouds would just cover the moon. She bit her lip in frustration. She didn't dare leave the shadows until the moon was obscured, and she must at least be across the courtyard before the guard rounded the north wall. She couldn't chance his being in the courtyard for the short time it would take her to get around the curve of the road.

Only three minutes to go. With one hand she tugged at the collar of her turtleneck sweater beneath the dark jacket while she clutched a coil of rope in the other. Move, damn you, she commanded the clouds. With maddening slowness, they drifted across the bright sphere, bringing the welcome darkness.

She flew out of the shadows like an arrow shot from a battlement in the chateau long ago, the rubber soles of her tennis shoes skimming over the rough cobbles with sure swiftness. By the time she reached the road she had only one minute to go before the guard would reappear, and already those blasted clouds were rolling through the skies as if fleeing the moon.

She streaked down the road, her braid flying out in back of her and her breath laboring in her lungs as she raced the cloud that could mean her escape or capture. She lost. She was a full fifty yards from the curve in the road when the moonlight suddenly flooded the road with the clarity of daylight. She felt the remaining breath leave her body, and she hesitated for a moment, as if that moonlight were an actual blow striking her. Lord, it was as bright as a spotlight, and the guard should be rounding the wall right now.

She hadn't thought she could go any faster, but the sudden burst of adrenaline that panic released proved her wrong. Let him be late, she prayed frantically, or let him be thinking of something else. Let him stop for a cigarette, or be looking anywhere but at the road. At any moment she expected to hear a shout and the sound of feet pounding heavily on the cobblestones behind her, but there was no sound except the sharp gasps of her own breathing. Then she'd rounded the curve in the road and was out of sight of the chateau!

Relief washed over her with a force that made her head swim. The first difficulty was overcome and she was on her way. She slowed her steps and then came to a complete halt. Her heart was pounding painfully in her breast and her knees felt weak as butter from reaction. Now that the first bit was out of the way she had to regain control of her nerves, twitching from the tension produced by the precarious cloud cover. There was still the checkpoint to get past and the rest of the road to the valley to cross before she was free.

Her pace slowed to a walk, and she hugged the inner side of the road, taking as much shelter as she could from the foliage on the side of the cliff. Heaven knew there was little enough to hug, she thought dispiritedly. The road seemed to be cut out of the mountain itself here—a bluff on one side, a sloping verge of perhaps five or six yards on the other side. From the edge of the verge it was a sheer drop to the valley below. But the verge was the key to her escape. She'd noticed there was a sparse straggle of trees on it near the checkpoint. With any luck she'd be able to use them as cover to slip past the chain link barricade across the road. Despite the moonlight, they should provide enough shadow for her to avoid being seen if she were careful. But that steeply sloping terrain was going to prove tricky. On her previous reconnaissance she'd detected little or no ground cover on the verge, and keeping her footing on an incline that steep until she reached the stand of pines was going to be nearly impossible. Her lips curved in a wry smile as she recalled her words to Jared only two weeks ago. Surefooted or not, she might well fall off this bloody mountain.

Well, that was why she'd brought the rope and the grappling hook, wasn't it? She could secure the rope around her waist and use the grappling hook on the trees, working her way from one to another across that sloping verge until she was past the checkpoint and it was safe to crawl back up on the road.

She'd been expecting it, but her heart still lurched when she came around the bend and saw the brilliant glow of the Coleman lanterns about fifty yards ahead. She instinctively shrank closer to the bluff while her gaze swiftly searched the scene ahead for an alternate route that wouldn't be as risky.

Two steel posts anchored the chain barrier stretched across the road. And the two guards who patrolled it were lounging on the bluff side of the road playing cards, leaning against the padded seats of their overturned motorcycles. She could hear their voices in the clear mountain air, and it gave her a little shock. They sounded so close she might have been right next to them. At least their lanterns were on the bluff side of the road, and if their game was interesting enough, it might take their attention off any noise she might make as she crawled past them. It was difficult to tell from this distance, but she didn't think they were the same guards who had brought her back to the chateau yesterday. In fact, neither one was familiar to her, and she'd thought she'd run across every security guard on the place at one time or another in the past two weeks.

Well, she couldn't stay here all night gawking at them. It was obvious the physical setup hadn't altered, and she was just going to have to keep to her original plan. She took the rope and grappling hook from her shoulder and checked the knot she'd tied in the steel loop of the hook to make sure it was tight, then dropped the grappling hook on the ground while she knotted the other end about her waist with equal care.

There was a burst of laughter from the men playing cards, and it caused her to jump with surprise. She drew a deep breath and forced herself to relax. Easy. This was just a piece of cake, remember? She was going to have to be very cool and certain in the next few minutes, and unsteady nerves would not help her.

She picked up the grappling hook and waited patiently until the clouds once more obscured the moon before dashing across the road and crouching on the edge of the verge for a moment. Then she slowly slid down onto the verge itself, carefully holding on to the trunk of the tree closest to the road. Oh, Lord, it was going to be worse than she'd thought. The earth slid out from under her, and she had to clutch desperately at the pine to keep from sliding with it. The ground seemed to be composed of nothing but loose dirt and shale—it was a wonder it even supported the scraggly pines that bordered the road. Still holding the trunk of the tree with one arm, she cautiously brought the grappling hook into play, reaching as far as she could and fastening it to the tree nearest her. Thank heaven the distance between most of the trees wasn't over two or three feet. It was a relatively simple matter to slip the hook around each slender trunk and then pull herself painstakingly hand over hand to the tree itself.

Once she became accustomed to the tempo of the procedure, her progress was much more rapid, and if she hadn't needed to be stealthy, she'd have been able to cover the fifty yards or so in a relatively short time. As it was, it took her almost twenty minutes to draw even with the barricade. She paused for a minute to catch her breath and wipe her chafed hands on her jeans before taking a fresh grip on the rope. With only the width of the road separating her from the two guards, she could feel her breath constrict in her lungs and the muscles of her stomach knot with tension. She could practically hear them breathe, she thought nervously. One false move and they'd be sure to hear her and react with the efficient swiftness Betz's security men always displayed.

But there wasn't going to be a false move. All she needed to do was to continue as she'd started, and in a few minutes she'd be safe. With the utmost caution she negotiated the next two trees, and she was past the checkpoint! Only a few yards past it, but it was a victory nonetheless.

Her swift surge of triumph was abruptly stemmed as she disengaged the hook and prepared to move on. The closest pine was over four yards away! The shock and dismay she felt almost caused her to let go of the tree she was clinging to. There was no possibility she'd be able to lean that far to slip the hook around the trunk. Damn it, just when she was almost home free. She bit her lips, anxiously trying to think of a way out. There was only one, and it was so risky that she hesitated to attempt it. She'd have to toss the hook and hope to encircle the base of the pine. In the darkness her chances of succeeding weren't all that great, and even if she did, the noise might give her away. Well, she really had no choice.

She just wished that she'd paid more attention when Tyler had wanted to teach her the fine art of pitching horseshoes, that weekend at the farm.

Her eyes straining in the darkness to gauge the distance, she balanced the hook in her hand as if it were a boomerang. Then, with a murmured prayer on her lips, she let the hook fly through the air. Had she made it?

But suddenly it no longer mattered. If the loud clang as the hook hit the shale hadn't given her away, the minor rockslide that resulted certainly had.

"What the hell was that?" One of the guards jumped to his feet, grabbing for a lantern.

There was nothing left to do but run for it. Her hands ripping frantically at the knot at her waist, she scrambled to her feet and lurched forward, trying desperately to regain the road.

Strangely, she didn't hear the crash of the shot until after she felt the first burning pain rip through her. She knew an instant of wild regret, more poignant than anything she'd ever experienced. Then there was only stark terror as she pitched forward, rolling like a broken toy down the sloping incline and off the edge of the cliff into the darkness beyond.

"Dr. Ryker, are you awake? It's essential that I speak to you." The knocking on his door was repeated with a persistence that belied the politeness of Betz's words.

How the hell could he help but be awake? Jared sat up in bed and leaned over to the bedside table to switch on the lamp. He'd just begun to drop off when Betz had started that damned knocking, and being wakened didn't improve a disposition that was on the raw anyway. "Come in, Betz. It had better be 'essential.'"

"I think you know by now I'd never disturb you for anything that wasn't extremely important." There was a touch of indignation in his ponderous voice.

"Get on with it, Betz," Jared said wearily. "You're here now. Let's have it."

"I'm afraid you may be quite upset, Dr. Ryker. There's been a slight difficulty regarding Miss Orlinov."

The impatience and annoyance vanished as the anxiety that was always latent in him these days surfaced rapidly. "Slight difficulty?" His voice was carefully neutral, his gaze sharp as a laser. "And just what do you consider slight, Betz?"

"She's been shot." Then, as Jared inhaled sharply and his face turned white, he continued hurriedly. "It's only a flesh wound in the shoulder. Liston assures me there was no serious damage done."

Jared threw back the covers and leaped out of bed, his every move charged with electricity. "Where is she?"

"He didn't intend to hit her—it was only meant to be a warning shot. He was startled when she appeared so suddenly at the checkpoint."

"The checkpoint? Is that where she is?" Why the hell hadn't he realized she'd try something like this? She'd been almost feverishly gay at dinner, and that should have signaled him that she was hiding something. Now she'd been hurt, and who knew how badly? My God, what if the bullet had severed an artery? She could bleed to death before he could even get there.

Betz was nodding. "Liston radioed word to me from the checkpoint by mobile phone and I dispatched the van to bring her back to the chateau." He paused. "I told them to wait to transport her until you arrived on the scene.

Jared grabbed a shirt and pants from the armoire. "I'll need the medical bag you'll find in the closet in the bathroom," he said crisply. "You have the jeep waiting?"

Betz moved obediently toward the door of the master bath. "Yes, of course. This is all very regrettable, Dr. Ryker. It *was* an accident, you realize."

"It may be more regrettable than you know." Jared's voice was icy, but there was sheer savagery in his granite-hard face. "Because if she's really badly hurt, I'm going to throw your man Liston off this son of a bitch of a mountain. I just may do it anyway. And then I'll start on you, Betz." He turned and left the bedroom, striding through the corridors and down the stairs.

The jeep was in the courtyard as Betz had promised. Jared looked grim as he swung up into the passenger seat. He drew a deep, calming breath. He mustn't give in to this rage that was tearing through him. He'd need all the cool steadiness he could muster when he saw how badly she was hurt.

Betz came hurrying out the courtyard door, carefully placed the brown cowhide medical bag he was carrying in the back, and slid into the driver's seat. "Sorry to have kept you waiting. I took the precaution of asking Dr. Jeffers to fly in immediately in case he was needed."

Jared tensed. "You told me it was only a flesh wound."

"I'm sure it is," Betz said quickly as he started the engine and put the jeep in gear. "It's just a precaution, Dr. Ryker."

"It'd better be, Betz," Jared said softly, his tone as menacing as a cocked pistol. "If I were you, I'd be praying very hard that it is."

The security man shrugged. He reversed the jeep with precision and drove out the arched gate of the courtyard. "In a few minutes you'll be able to judge for yourself."

The checkpoint was teeming with activity and lights when they rounded the curve. Betz halted the jeep directly before the van and was immediately approached by a tall young man in a leather jacket who burst hurriedly into speech. "It wasn't our fault, Mr. Betz. She hopped up out of the trees and surprised us. We didn't even know who she was. All we saw was a shadow."

"And do you always shoot at shadows?" Jared bit out.

The man moistened his lips nervously as his gaze took in Jared's taut face and blazing eyes. "Not always, sir. But in this case we were told to shoot first and ask questions later, because your safety was paramount. We were only following orders, Dr. Ryker."

"Where is she?" He had to make sure that Tania was all right before he gave himself the pleasure of taking the man apart limb from limb.

The man answered quickly. "We've put her in the back of the van. I've rigged up a bandage for her shoulder, and the bleeding has stopped. She's unconscious now, but she fainted only when I was applying the bandage." He turned. "I'll take you to her."

"Let's go," Jared said crisply. He got out of the jeep and strode rapidly toward the back of the van.

When Jared reached the back of the van, one glance told him that Betz's very valuable man was extremely close to being permanently mutilated. "My God, her clothes are torn to shreds. What the hell have you done to her? You lying bastard, if I find out you've raped her, I'll chop you into little pieces." He dropped to his knees beside Tania. "Where did she get all these bruises?"

"We didn't touch her," Liston protested desperately. He swallowed hard and then proceeded more calmly. "Those are rope burns. When she was shot, she rolled down the incline and over the edge of the cliff. She'd been using a grappling hook on the trees, to inch her way past the checkpoint, and the rope was still knotted about her waist when she rolled over the edge of the cliff. The rope kept her from falling to the valley below, but naturally the jerk bruised her quite a bit." He tried to smile. "Donalson and I tried to be as careful as we could when we pulled her back to the verge, but there wasn't any way we could prevent her from getting a little scraped. She was lucky as hell to come out of it as well as she did."

Lucky. Jared felt the muscles of his stomach tighten at the vivid picture Liston's terse words evoked. Tania dangling hundreds of feet in the air from a slender rope and two trigger-happy idiots the only hope she had of survival. It made him sick even to think about it. Lord, yes, she'd been lucky.

"You say she was still conscious when you were bandaging her wound?" Jared asked thickly. He hoped not. It must have been sheer hell for her if she'd been totally aware during that nightmarish experience.

Liston nodded eagerly. "She was conscious the entire time until we were trying to get her jacket off. She was even able to help a little while we were hauling her up the cliff." He knelt beside Ryker and pushed aside the torn sweater to reveal a crude bandage fashioned of brown plaid flannel, obviously torn from a shirt. "See, the bleeding's stopped entirely. The bullet just grazed her shoulder, clean as a whistle."

"Get your hands off her!" Liston jumped as if he'd been flicked with a whip and backed hurriedly away. Jared drew a deep breath and tried to submerge the anger that had suddenly exploded. "Just get out of here, Liston. Now!"

The guard didn't have to be told twice. As the man jumped out of the van Ryker didn't give him a second glance. His gaze was fixed intently on Tania's shoulder.

"Clean as a whistle," he repeated disgustedly. "She'll be lucky if she doesn't get blood poisoning," Jared said grimly, carefully cutting away the flannel bandage. His hands were remarkably steady, he noticed absently. It was a wonder, when he was shaking so inside. He hadn't felt as helpless as this since the night Lita died. But he wasn't helpless now. He had knowledge and experience on his side. He had to remember that. He hadn't been able to help Lita then, but he could help Tania now.

He soon discovered Liston was right. Though the wound looked ugly and inflamed, the bullet had just grazed the fleshy part of the shoulder. He breathed a sigh of relief as he quickly removed the bandage and reached for an antiseptic. He carefully cleaned the wound before rebandaging it with sterile gauze and taping it firmly.

"That's all I can do for her now. I'll give her a shot to ease the pain, and antibiotic and tetanus injections. After that it's up to your doctor to do his stuff. Now let's get her back to the chateau. Tell the driver I want the ride to be pure velvet. If he jars her even a little, I'll break his neck. Understand?"

"You needn't worry. I've already warned him to be most careful." Betz disappeared from view, and a moment later Jared could hear his voice at the front of the van.

Taking off his jacket, Jared put it carefully over Tania. He barely heard the van doors close as he drew her into his arms so that she was lying across his lap and cradled against the cushion of his shoulder.

She was very light, yet there was a solid warmth about her that was vaguely comforting. It reminded him of the vitality and strength that usually glowed from her like an aura, and God knew he needed that memory now. His arms tightened about her protectively as the driver started the engine and then drove slowly and cautiously up the road toward the chateau.

It was strange to experience this feeling of belonging to another human being after all those years of standing alone. Strange and a little painful. He wasn't sure he liked it. The emotion had too many sharp edges, and it would probably take time to round them off before he'd feel comfortable with it. Well, he had all the time he needed, and he'd better start adjusting now, because he knew it wasn't going to go away.

He had called it an obsession, and it certainly had been that. She had amused and challenged him at every turn, sparking off him like a small firecracker, arousing him to sexual frenzy one moment and touching off that melting tenderness in him the next. He hadn't really allowed himself to think beyond their time together at the chateau. Perhaps he'd been a little afraid to face the commitment he'd seen glimmering on the horizon the first night he'd met her. Now that commitment wasn't on the horizon, it was here in his arms. The knowledge had exploded within him with the same force as the bullet that had struck her, destroying all the unessentials as if they'd never been.

"Jared."

It was a mere ribbon of a whisper, but he heard it, and his gaze flew down to meet the brilliant darkness of her own. The vitality of her expressive eyes made the fragility and pallor of her face even more apparent, and he felt a thrill of fear course through him. "Are you in any pain?" he asked quickly.

She thought a moment. "A little."

"I've given you a shot. You should be more comfortable very soon."

"I'm comfortable now." She nestled closer to him. "I feel so warm and safe." She shivered. "I was frightened, Jared. I don't think I've ever been as frightened in my life." Her words were becoming slurred as the sedative took effect, and they were spoken with a childlike simplicity. "Hanging there in the darkness knowing—"

"Don't think about it," he said huskily. "It's over and you're safe." His arms tightened about her. "You'll always be safe now."

 # LOVESWEPT

Love Stories you'll never forget by authors you'll always remember

☐	21603	**Heaven's Price #1** Sandra Brown	$1.95
☐	21604	**Surrender #2** Helen Mittermeyer	$1.95
☐	21600	**The Joining Stone #3** Noelle Berry McCue	$1.95
☐	21601	**Silver Miracles #4** Fayrene Preston	$1.95
☐	21605	**Matching Wits #5** Carla Neggers	$1.95
☐	21606	**A Love for All Time #6** Dorothy Garlock	$1.95
☐	21609	**Hard Drivin' Man #10** Nancy Carlson	$1.95
☐	21610	**Beloved Intruder #11** Noelle Berry McCue	$1.95
☐	21611	**Hunter's Payne #12** Joan J. Domning	$1.95
☐	21618	**Tiger Lady #13** Joan Domning	$1.95
☐	21613	**Stormy Vows #14** Iris Johansen	$1.95
☐	21614	**Brief Delight #15** Helen Mittermeyer	$1.95
☐	21616	**A Very Reluctant Knight #16** Billie Green	$1.95
☐	21617	**Tempest at Sea #17** Iris Johansen	$1.95
☐	21619	**Autumn Flames #18** Sara Orwig	$1.95
☐	21620	**Pfarr Lake Affair #19** Joan Domning	$1.95
☐	21621	**Heart on a String #20** Carla Neggars	$1.95
☐	21622	**The Seduction of Jason #21** Fayrene Preston	$1.95
☐	21623	**Breakfast In Bed #22** Sandra Brown	$1.95
☐	21624	**Taking Savannah #23** Becky Combs	$1.95
☐	21625	**The Reluctant Lark #24** Iris Johansen	$1.95

<u>**Prices and availability subject to change without notice.**</u>

Buy them at your local bookstore or use this handy coupon for ordering:

Bantam Books, Inc., Dept. SW, 414 East Golf Road, Des Plaines, Ill. 60016

Please send me the books I have checked above. I am enclosing
$_____ (please add $1.25 to cover postage and handling). Send
check or money order—no cash or C.O.D.'s please.

Mr/Ms_____

Address_____

City/State_____ Zip_____

SW—3/85

Please allow four to six weeks for delivery. This offer expires 9/85.

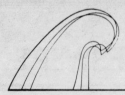

LOVESWEPT

Love Stories you'll never forget by authors you'll always remember